RED CURTAIN

RED CURTAIN

DON SMITH

CUTTING EDGE

ISBN-13: 978-1-954840-40-9

Published by
Cutting Edge Books
PO Box 8212
Calabasas, CA 91372
www.cuttingedgebooks.com

CHAPTER ONE

THERE WERE ONLY two of us left in the Sherman family—myself and my younger brother. He had been captured in Korea ; when he returned eighteen months later, he was minus his legs. The Red medico had decided that the surest way to cure frostbite was by amputation. No, I had no particular love for the Communists.

That was why, one beautiful April evening, I was walking along Paris's Avenue Foch to Dmitri Smirnoff's apartment near the Bois. He had called earlier and said he had heard of something which I might find interesting. "It might even amuse you," he added. "You are not very fond of the Communists, if I recall." So I decided to see him that night.

His greeting was warm if a bit perfunctory and as I sat down in the well-worn but extremely comfortable leather armchair, I noticed him steal a quick glance at his watch.

"A most unusual client called on me this morning, Philip," he explained without further preliminary, "and I want you to meet him. He is coming at seven and I would like to tell you about him before he arrives. When you've heard the story you will understand why I asked you to come around." He sat down at his desk and, since it seemed to be expected of me, I sipped my drink in silence and watched him.

Dmitri was one of the most well-known lawyers on the Continent and was, I happened to know, a long way past seventy. As I looked at him now, I hoped the years would treat me as lightly. He was not fleshy and there wasn't a loose wrinkle on his rosy, cherubic face. His intensely brown, round eyes were clear, and topping all was a magnificent flowing mane of silver-gray hair. As always, he was impeccably dressed; tonight he was wearing a beautifully cut dinner jacket. In the lapel was a blood red carnation.

"This man," he said finally, "claims to be an official of the Soviet Ministry of Foreign Trade attached to the Russian Embassy in Belgium."

He paused, a little dramatically I thought, for his statement to sink in. I knew Dmitri had been born in Russia and that he had left that country during the Revolution. He had subsequently acquired French citizenship and settled down in Paris. But I had never heard him express any particular feelings one way or the other about the Soviet regime. In the eyes of the Communists, he was undoubtedly still considered a White Russian and I began to understand his excitement when one of their officials had come to seek his legal advice. But why he thought the story would interest me—

"His credentials seem authentic," Dmitri's voice broke into my thoughts, "although I haven't had time to verify them. One letter is from the Ministry of Foreign Trade in Moscow authorizing him to dispose of certain unspecified rare metals on behalf of the Soviet Government. These metals—or rather this metal; it appears there was only one —he has sold on the various free markets of Western Europe, and the proceeds have been deposited by him in the USSR Embassy account in Bern."

Again Dmitri paused, and this time I ventured: "Gold?"

"No, Philip. Platinum."

"Platinum? Yes, I've heard there was a lot floating around recently. So it came from Russia?"

"Apparently so. However, this Monsieur Englhardt—his name is Nicholas Englhardt—mentioned such an astronomical amount that I consider it slightly incredible."

"You mustn't forget he's not representing an individual firm," I pointed out. "He represents the whole country. Russia is one of the world's largest producers of platinum, and if she decided to dump even a six months' supply on the world market..." I shrugged.

"Perhaps you are right. Anyway, that doesn't concern us now." Dmitri hunched over his desk and, his intense eyes fixed on mine, continued, "Englhardt explained that he was able to wangle favorable exchange rates when he sold the platinum. And he reached the total sum his government expected from the sale before he'd sold it all."

"In other words, if the USSR set a price of so many roubles for the lot, and Englhardt was able to find a buyer who wanted to get rid of roubles—he made a deal."

Dmitri nodded. "And he claims that the metal left over after the sales is his commission."

"Commission!" I snorted. "How capitalistic these Communists have suddenly become!"

"I agree. But no doubt he thought that if he came to me and openly admitted that he had embezzled this metal I would have shown him the door." Dmitri chuckled. "And though I know I should have, I'm not sure that I would have. My family owned a good deal of property in Russia before the Bolsheviks seized everything."

"Which is obviously why he came to you. You have a name I'm sure the Reds know, even if they no longer respect it. And, being who you are, your client felt that if you decided he was a crook, you wouldn't turn him over to the Soviets."

Dmitri nodded and again glanced at his watch. "But we must hurry. This ten percent amounts, he claims, to 285 kilos—"

"Whew!" I whistled soundlessly. "Why that's..." I paused and tried to recall the present price of platinum.

"Almost a million dollars," Dmitri explained. "I checked with my bankers this morning."

My curiosity was not only kindled now, it was crackling. He went on. "Englhardt has asked me to find a responsible business man to dispose of this metal for him. He is already known to the principal platinum buyers in Europe, and cannot go to them and sell the metal for his own account. And if he claims it is for the Russian Government, he is afraid that one of them might check with his superiors."

"Which knocks his commission story into a cocked hat."

"Exactly. But when I pointed this out to him, he explained that the attitude in the lower echelons of the ministry is that anything extra which can be squeezed out of the capitalists is legitimate personal gain."

"He must be crazy!"

"I'm afraid I may have suggested the same thing, because he stood up and said that if. I wasn't interested, he'd go elsewhere. I told him to sit down."

"Then what?"

"The man who does the selling for him will deposit the pro-ceeds in a numbered account in a Swiss bank. Which account, I presume, is Englhardt's."

"And for this?"

"He will receive ten percent commission plus expenses which he will deduct from each sale."

"Where is the stuff now?"

"Switzerland. But if you accept, I'll let him explain the details."

"Now, just one minute. What makes—"

"I immediately thought of you. You are not French, and therefore are not subject to our currency restrictions. You know the European commercial world like the back of your hand. And I remember your feelings toward the Communists."

I sat back and slowly tapped the glass with a finger. Dmitri was right on all three counts, of course. Particularly the last. A crippled brother was the biggest reason, and now the new Russian economic drive was seriously affecting my own business affairs.

But on the other hand, ten percent of a million dollars is a lot of money in any currency, and if this man Englhardt was willing to pay that to someone to dispose of a commodity which was as easy to sell as gold—well, there must be certain risks which I didn't know about yet.

"You think he's on the level?" I inquired finally. "As you said, the whole thing sounds more than a little incredible."

Dmitri shrugged. "Who knows? But you must admit it is an intriguing story. And what have you to lose? Englhardt is not asking you to put up anything, so if you find you don't like the looks of it, all you have to do is walk out. And if everything is as he claims it to be, you stand to earn quite a lot of money."

I gave him a long quizzical look. "Dmitri," I said, "I have a sneaking suspicion that there is more than monetary profit behind your suggestion that I go into this—to say the least— highly questionable deal."

"Of course!" He sat back and laughed. "But please don't misunderstand me. Once I have introduced you to him, I want no part of it. I only wish to prove a point—that Communism, like Fascism and Nazism, is not here to stay. And in Englhardt I hope we have discovered the first crack in the Kremlin wall. When these party *fonctionnaires* begin to feather their own nests with foreign assets, it is obvious they don't have a great deal of confidence in their future, either nationally or personally. Oh yes, my dear Philip! I'm going to be very disappointed if this fellow turns out to be just another crack-brained confidence man!"

"That's all very well for you," I observed drily. "But just exactly what is my legal position if I do go into this thing?"

Dmitri shrugged again. "A government official of the USSR comes to you and asks you to sell a certain commodity. Possibly the arrangements are a little unusual, but then we all know that the Russians are highly secretive in their commercial affairs. How are you to know that the commodity was stolen or embezzled? Particularly since the man attempts to establish his true identity."

"Which might be a perfect defense," I admitted, "provided I don't try to use it behind the Iron Curtain."

At that moment the butler entered and handed Dmitri a card. And as he glanced at it, I looked at my watch. It was exactly seven o'clock. I was to learn that everything Nicholas Englhardt did in his life was with the same meticulous, stop-watch precision.

My first impression of him was one of pleasant surprise; I liked his appearance. Everything about him was large, but not gross. He was tall and powerfully built; when I stood up to be introduced, his intensely blue, calm eyes were above mine, and I'm six feet. He had very large hands and wrists, and it would not have surprised me to learn that he'd been a professional boxer or wrestler. He stood very straight with a military erectness and I fully expected him to click his heels as we shook hands. If I had not been certain that Dmitri could recognize a fellow Russian when he saw one, I would have suspected that this man and the *Wehrmacht* were not unacquainted. And I could understand now why he felt it necessary to find an intermediary to dispose of his loot. Anyone who met Nicholas Englhardt was not likely soon to forget that imposing, almost overbearing figure.

After we had sat down, Dmitri spoke to him for some time in Russian. I presumed he was explaining that I might be interested in his offer as from time to time I caught Englhardt carefully looking me over.

I was beginning to hope that he spoke another language besides his own when Dmitri turned to me and said, "I must apologize, Philip, but Mr. Englhardt asked me to tell him about you, and he says that since his English is inadequate—"

I raised a protesting hand. "I understand. Carry on."

"I am sorry," Englhardt spoke up. "I speak German, French, Turkish, Serbian—"

I laughed. "And you appear able to handle English."

"With your assistance, I shall improve. Mr. Smirnoff tells me that you are interested in my proposition."

"Interested, certainly. But there are a few questions before I definitely commit myself."

"Of course."

"In the first place—and you must excuse me for being extremely blunt, but that is my nature—was this metal stolen?"

A wide smile broke across his pleasant features. "No, Mr. Sherman. One cannot very well steal 285 kilos of platinum. It is not something one can slip into one's pocket while the owner is not looking."

This man's English, I decided, was somewhat more than adequate. I continued, "Let me put it this way: was it obtained by false pretences or embezzlement?"

And although I was certain that he understood perfectly well what I meant, he turned to Dmitri and asked him to translate into Russian.

"I presumed Mr. Smirnoff had explained where this metal came from," he said finally. "As an international business man you will understand that in transferring large sums of money from one continental currency to another, it is sometimes possible to gain on the exchange. That is, if one has patience and friends."

"Of course. So by getting favorable exchange rates each time you sold some platinum, it was not necessary to sell all of it to make up the sum your government expected."

"That is correct."

Slowly, I nodded. I knew that in these days of soft and hard currencies this was standard business procedure. If a man had hard Canadian dollars and wished to buy soft French francs he would naturally buy them in Switzerland and receive twenty percent more for his money than he would if he bought them in Paris. If you had a substantial stake to start with and, as Englhardt pointed out, friends, you could make a lot of money. Of course, you could also lose. In which case, Englhardt would probably be breaking stones in Siberia—if he were lucky.

The only catch was that he was not a private citizen speculating with his own funds. He was—or claimed to be—a government official, and the capital he'd been manipulating was government money.

So what sort of an accessory did that make me if I helped him get rid of the metal he'd held back for himself?

Or was he just a contact man sent out to enmesh Dmitri or me—or both of us—in some darkly sinister Communist intrigue?

"And your government," I went on, "is not interested in the fact that you have made what you call a commission?"

He showed his powerful teeth in an innocent grin. "Why should they be aware of it? We do not keep books in these transactions, Mr. Sherman."

"Naturally." I returned his smile with the swift thought that this strange, seemingly ingenuous character made Washington five-percenters look like chicken feeders. "Where is the metal now?"

"I'm afraid, Mr. Sherman, you will have to decide whether or not you are coming in with me before we can discuss details."

"Fair enough. Well, on the facts as I know them, I'm your man. I have no compunction whatever about helping get the commission you have extracted from your ministry. In fact, for various reasons, I'll enjoy it. Provided, that is, I don't end up in jail or with a knife stuck in my back." I turned to Dmitri. "However, I want you to make this very clear to Mr. Englhardt in his own language. I don't like Communists, and if at any time I suspect that I'm being used as a tool to further his country's ambitions, I shall not only back out, but I will do everything in my power to spike his little game."

Englhardt didn't wait for the translation. "I am pleased that you are being so frank with me," he said. "And I have a feeling that you and I are going to get along very well together."

After a disturbed, dream-filled night in which mountains of platinum played no small part, the following morning I found myself eyeing the telephone long before ten o'clock, when Nicholas was supposed to call. Even in the cold reasonableness of morning, I was determined to go through with the deal if the risks were not too obviously inacceptable. The Transeastern Supply Company of New York and Paris —of which I was not only the director but the principal shareholder—was paying its way, but the situation in Africa and the Near East was slowly drying up some of our more lucrative markets. The Russian carpet-baggers had arrived and offered everything from consumer goods to ships at ridiculous prices and quarter-century credit. These new countries would wake up—provided they didn't go Communist first—and find it hadn't been Santa Claus driving the droshky. But I was afraid that before that day of enlightenment arrived, companies like the Transeastern would have withered down to the roots.

I was beginning to believe in poetic justice when the telephone rang. Automatically I glanced at the clock; it was exactly ten A.M. Englhardt asked me where we could meet in private and I suggested my apartment. He immediately agreed and said that he would be right over.

He came in with his great long strides, shook hands and walked over to one of the windows. "You have a nice place here," he said, his restless eyes surveying the building across the court.

"Not bad." And then I realized what was worrying him. "Care to see the rest of it?"

"With pleasure."

I showed him the other rooms, even the closets, and when we got to the kitchen I was glad the maid had gone to the market.

It wouldn't have surprised me if he had tipped up some of the paintings to look for hidden microphones. When, finally, he was assured we were indeed alone, he relaxed and sat down.

"And now, Mr. Sherman," he said, pulling out a thick, well-worn wallet, "let us discuss business."

He extracted several official-looking papers from the wallet and handed them to me one by one. The first was the letter Dmitri had described authorizing him to sell precious metals. It bore an official Soviet seal; attached to it was Englhardt's photograph. The second letter was from the Embassy empowering Englhardt to act on behalf of the USSR Government in regard to some trade delegation. There were three or four other letters along similar lines, all bearing the government seal.

He then showed me an International driving license and what he explained was a Red Army discharge certificate bearing his photograph which obviously had been taken some years previously. He had been a colonel in the tank corps, he said, wounded twice and had seen action on such gory fronts as Stalingrad.

"These are very interesting," I said, after spreading them out on my desk. "There's only one thing missing."

"What is that?" His eyebrows lifted.

Without answering, I unlocked a drawer in the desk and took out my passport and dropped it on the table beside him.

"Ah yes, my passport," he said, casually picking mine up and thumbing through the pages. "Mine is at the Embassy in Brussels. You must understand that we Russians are not permitted to travel at will. If I wish to leave the country in which I am stationed, I must give my reasons to the Ambassador. If he is satisfied that my request is justified—and believe me it would only be for official business—he gives me my passport."

"I understand. How then were you able to cross into France and come to Paris?"

Englhardt sat back in his chair and gave me his pleasant smile. "You are more of a lawyer than our friend, Mr. Smirnoff."

"I have to be." I matched his smile. "I'm risking more."

From another pocket he got a small green folder and handed it to me. It was a Belgium *carte d'identité* in the name of Nicholas Hammert. It bore Englhardt's photograph and had been issued six months previously.

"That cost me one hundred thousand Belgian francs," he said, drily.

"You could have bought one here for a fraction of that."

"And be picked up the first time I crossed a frontier. No, believe me, I know. A Belgian *carte* is the best. And that one—" he leaned over and tapped the document with a long finger "—is authentic. That name is on file at the Hotel de Ville in Brussels."

"And did the previous owner resemble you?"

He showed his powerful teeth. "There was no previous owner, Mr. Sherman. But there was a false birth certificate issued from a Belgian town whose birth records had been destroyed by bombing during the war."

"You are very thorough."

"I have to be. I hope that you are also."

Again he picked up my passport. "Now that I have explained who I am, if you please, I would like you to describe for me your—what do you call it—your background. I see here that you were born in New York forty-one years ago. I congratulate you. I thought you were considerably younger. Are you married?"

"Not yet."

"Any immediate family?"

"Only a brother. He lives in California and is, ah, a cripple."

"War?"

"Korea."

"I see." And then a moment later : "Mr. Sherman, perhaps it would be as well to tell you now that I am not a Communist. I have a feeling that we will get along better if you know that."

"As a matter of fact, I was waiting to ask you that very question. Then how is it that you have a government position?"

"I am a Russian." It was wonderful the way he seemed to pull himself up in his chair and with blazing eyes roll out that simple statement. "I love my country. I have fought for her, and will again if she is in danger. But…" His voice drifted off and he seemed to be fumbling for words as his eyes left mine and turned towards the window.

"You don't like the gang who is running things now, is that it?"

"You are right." His eyes picked up mine again. "Those *schouft*—" of all his languages I was to learn he swore only in German "—are ruining us. If they would take their stupid, covetous eyes off other countries and let us work in peace for ourselves, we would become the greatest nation in history!"

"You might have something there," I said quietly, sensing an argument building up. I was more interested at that moment in his platinum than in his political views. "So you have decided not to wait for them to see reason but to protect your own future while the opportunity is available."

"Correct, Mr. Sherman. With your assistance I am going to make ten million dollars!" His voice began to boom.

Shrewdly, and with no little disappointment, I stared at him and wondered if Dmitri Smirnoff hadn't after all introduced me to one of those colorfully crazy White Russians who are unfortunately disappearing from the European scene. I recalled the lawyer's observation that perhaps we'd discovered a crack in the Kremlin wall. I hoped the crack didn't turn out to be in this man's head.

"Ten million," I said slowly. "I didn't realize you had that much platinum."

"Platinum!" Englhardt dismissed it with a wave of his enormous hand. "That is only the beginning. Look at this." Again he dug into the wallet which doubled for a briefcase and unfolded another letter. It instructed him to give thought to the sale of 24,000 typewriters and 18,000 cameras.

"With the money we get from the platinum we will form a company," he went on. "You will form the company and I will be the silent partner. Then, on behalf of the Russian Government, I will authorize the sale of these articles to you at a very low price. You will resell them on the world market and we will share the profits equally."

Slowly, I nodded. If this man were crazy, I was beginning to think, he was crazy like a fox.

"Were these machines made in Russia?" I asked.

"No, they are good German machines. Made in East Germany in factories which were dismantled after the war and moved from the Western Zone by the Russians. And later, Mr. Sherman, when we have built up capital, we'll deal in ships. Russia is in need of shipping and I will arrange it so that they are purchased through your company."

Carefully, I refolded his various papers and handed them back to him, my racing thoughts contemplating the fabulous opportunities this Russian giant was offering me. With an agent like him planted inside the USSR Ministry of Foreign Trade, the Transeastern Supply Company would certainly more than merely survive this period of politically inspired commercial nepotism. What an amazing coincidence that of all men he might have turned to, he had found me!

"When," I asked him, "do I pick up the platinum?"

CHAPTER TWO

THE FOLLOWING SATURDAY evening I was standing at the bar of the Palace Hotel in Lucerne. I had driven from Paris to Switzerland the day before and, following Englhardt's instructions, had parked my Mercedes 190 in a garage in Lausanne and hired a late model Buick from a car rental agency there. It would be more discreet, he had explained, if the car I used had Swiss license plates. Next, I had gone to the Lausanne branch of the Swiss bank and rented four large safe deposit boxes in my name and paid a year's rent in advance for them. Englhardt had given me a rough idea of the cubic measurement of the platinum and I made sure the four boxes between them would be more than sufficient to hold it as well as take its weight.

I glanced at my watch. It was five minutes to six and I asked the barman for another whisky. "Does it always rain in Lucerne?" I said.

"It is the spring, monsieur."

"And tomorrow?"

He shrugged. "It is said there will be sun."

"I hope so." Yes, I certainly did hope so, particularly if Englhardt had his platinum buried on some mountain side.

When he arrived, he stood in the entrance to the bar for a moment and casually surveyed the room. His eyes caught mine but with no sign of recognition, passed on. I turned back to my drink.

"A quarter of champagne, *garçon*." His voice was not far from my shoulder. The barman thumbed out the cork and filled a glass. "This *verdampt* weather!"

Casually I turned and smiled at him. "I was just saying the same thing," I said. "But George here tells me tomorrow it will be fine."

From the weather, we discussed the roads and the perils of Swiss alpine driving in spring and what one did during a rainy weekend in Lucerne. Finally, he invited me to have a drink and suggested we move over to a quiet corner by the fire. I accepted and he told the barman to bring the drinks over.

"Why the cloak and dagger approach?" I asked when we were alone.

"It is better that they believe we met casually."

I glanced nervously over my shoulder, fully expecting to find a gang of strong-arm MVD thugs panting down my neck. But with the exception of a group of elderly people in one corner and a gray-haired individual with a very expensive-looking girl friend in another, the place was deserted.

"Who do you mean, they?" I demanded in an undertone.

"Anyone who might have recognized me—or you," he explained.

I sat back and smiled with relief. "Give me time. I'll learn."

"You have the car?"

"Yes. It's in the hotel garage."

"Good."

"Want to see it?"

"No. Just tell me the license number and type."

I handed him the car's papers and he jotted down the license number on the back of an envelope. "Dark blue, 1955 sedan."

"That's right."

"I'll recognize it." He took a map of the district out of his pocket and unfolded it. "Do you know the country around here?"

"Reasonably well. Particularly the main highways."

"Tomorrow morning you will drive to Interlaken. Take the highway via Brunigpass and you will find the scenery delightful—"

"Provided I can see it."

"Yes. It's going to make things less pleasant if it is raining. However, when you get to Interlaken, drive along the north shore of lake Thuner-see towards Gunten. This is not the main highway but it is a good road. Exactly seven kilometers from Interlaken you will find a café on the side of the lake. It is not open yet, but in the summer it is a popular place to swim. Just west of the café are some trees. Follow the lane between the café and the trees until you reach the edge of the lake, turn to the right and park the car. The clump of trees will shelter you from the road. I suggest you take some sandwiches and a bottle of wine and have your lunch there. It is very pleasant."

"And if there are other cars around?"

"I doubt if there will be this time of the year. But, if there are, continue along the lane until you find a deserted spot. I shall arrive at two o'clock in the afternoon, and I shall be driving a 1954 Sunbeam with CD license plates."

"Color?"

"Black sedan."

"And?"

"Have your luggage compartment unlocked but not open and be ready to help me transfer the platinum."

I smiled. "This sounds a lot easier than I expected. I was afraid we might have to dig it out of some alpine cave."

"For you, it is simple." He made a wry face. "But it is going to take me most of tonight to dig the metal out of the wall of the apartment of the *chargé d'affaires* at the Embassy in Bern and carry it down to his car in the garage below."

I sat up. "You mean the *chargé d'affaires* knows about this?"

"Yes, Mr. Sherman. Without his assistance it would not have been possible for me to accumulate it."

"And you trust him?"

"He is to receive half the proceeds."

I was silent for some time. This piece of news I didn't like. I could understand Englhardt's actions—he was just a lesser official in the Ministry of Foreign Trade taking a cut out of a private deal he himself handled. But the *chargé d'affaires!* The man second only to the ambassador in an important post like Bern! Just what was Soviet officialdom coming to anyway? Or was I walking blindly into some fantastic Communist scheme? I began to wish I had Dmitri Smirnoff with me. I could use his advice.

"What's the trouble?" Englhardt finally asked. "You look worried."

"To be quite honest, I am. I wish you had told me in Paris there were others connected with this deal besides yourself."

"Does it matter?"

"Certainly. How do I know you haven't a string of accomplices stretching from here to the Kremlin?"

He smiled easily. "Take my word for it, there is not. I am not a fool."

"And why do you tell me about this man now?"

"For two reasons. First, you will have to deposit his share in a separate account, and secondly, I did not wish you to be surprised when you checked up on the owner of the diplomatic corps car I will have tomorrow."

"What makes you think I would?"

"In your place, Mr. Sherman, I would have."

"You play it close to the vest, don't you?"

"I don't believe I understand—"

"Let it go. As I said once before tonight, I'm learning. Does your colleague know about me?"

"No, and he has no interest."

"And you're sure he'll not weaken one day and turn you in?"

"He has a wife and four children."

"He might turn state's evidence and throw himself on the mercy of the court."

"In Russia, Mr. Sherman?"

The look he gave me made me feel a little juvenile and I remained silent. A moment later he called the barman over and asked for the bill. And after he'd paid it, he said, "My friend, his wife and I will leave the Embassy about eleven o'clock tomorrow morning and go into the country for a picnic. If it is still raining, we will go to an inn. When we have found a spot, I will leave them and come to meet you in his car. After we have transferred the metal, I will return and pick them up."

"Do I see you later?"

"No. I suggest you drive straight back here, make sure the car is locked in the garage and spend the night here. Monday morning, take the metal to Lausanne and place it in the bank."

I nodded. And that will be a good night's sleep, I thought, with a carload of platinum in the garage. I hoped it was fireproof.

"And when this is done," Englhardt went on, "go and see this man in Geneva." He extracted a card from his wallet and handed it to me. "Offer him twenty kilos, no more, at the market price. If he accepts, arrange to meet him at the bank in Lausanne and give him the metal only when you have received the money—in cash."

"Why only twenty kilos if he should want more?"

"The platinum market is very tender. We do not wish to depress prices by flooding it."

He stood up as I tucked the card away. "I'm sorry, but now I must leave you," he said pleasantly. We shook hands. "It has been an enjoyable hour and I have had a wonderful time practicing my English."

I glanced around to see if he was speaking for someone else's benefit. But we were still alone and I suddenly realized he was serious! What marvelous nerves this character has, I thought. Here he was on his way to the Russian Embassy where he planned to spend the night removing a quarter of a ton of hot platinum from inside the walls and then tomorrow driving gaily out for a picnic with it packed under the lunch basket. And yet he takes the time to tell me how he's enjoyed practicing his English!

I found myself beginning to like Englhardt.

I added another disturbed night to the debit balance of the platinum. By the time a misty dawn had turned the black surface of the lake into molten gunmetal, I had been chased by so many Cossacks over so many steppes, I decided it was time I did a little chasing myself.

As a result, it was not yet eight o'clock when I got the Buick out of the garage and had it filled with gas and oil. But instead of turning south for Interlaken, I took the highway to Bern. It had stopped raining and if the swirling mists, like phantom shrouds clinging to the hillsides, cleared away, it would be a nice day.

I reached Bern before ten and stopped at a kiosk and bought a street map of the city. I ordered coffee and rolls in a nearby café and looked up the address of the Russian Embassy in the telephone directory. I located the place on the map and studied the streets in that vicinity. The coffee was excellent, but my stomach was too full of nerves to find room for the creamy white rolls.

I drove along Brunnadernrain Strasse and slowly passed the entrance to the Embassy. A quick glance showed me that there were several buildings, and there was no way to tell in which the *chargé d'affaires* lived. I parked the car a couple of blocks away and walked back. Brunnadernrain Strasse was a wide, tree-lined avenue with little traffic and few pedestrians. My watch told me it was 10:45 and I stood there hesitating, feeling very conspicuous.

I followed the street away from the Embassy and looked for a café. But after two blocks and none in sight, I turned and retraced my steps. Out of an iron rubbish basket, I salvaged an old newspaper, shook out the dust and hoped that no Swiss burgher was watching me. About a hundred yards from the Embassy

I stopped, lit a cigarette, and opened the newspaper. A gendarme on his beat outside the Embassy entrance threw me a quick look and I proceeded to look fascinated by the news. It was eleven o'clock.

Ten minutes later I noticed a car circling the driveway inside the Embassy gates. I moved up the side road and buried my face in the paper. A few moments later the car passed along Brunnadernrain Strasse, driving fast. A man was behind the wheel and beside him sat a middle-aged woman with a bright scarf around her head. Englhardt—there was no mistaking that massive figure—was sitting in the back seat looking out the side window, his back toward me. The car was a Sunbeam and it was well down on the springs.

I gave them a full minute and returned to Brunnadernrain Strasse. The Sunbeam had disappeared and there was no sign of a car following. Out of the corner of my eye I noticed the gendarme approaching and I had a strong suspicion that he was going to speak to me. Casually, I folded the paper, glanced at my watch and walked towards him. I gave him a polite smile and kept on going. I could feel his speculative eyes boring into my back.

I felt a little foolish as I returned to the Buick. Everything had taken place as exactly as Englhardt had said. So what was I doing playing secret agent on a quiet Sunday morning in Bern? Served me right, I told myself, if that gendarme had picked me up for loitering suspiciously outside a foreign embassy. And what was I trying to prove? That Englhardt hadn't been caught during the night? Or that he really was bringing the platinum from the Russian Embassy?

I started the car and admitted to myself that I didn't know. What I was beginning to know was that I'd be very glad when that damn platinum was finally disposed of. I wondered how long it took to grow an ulcer.

I parked outside a small restaurant, went in, had a drink and ordered some sandwiches made up. I took my time. If the

Sunbeam was driving toward Interlaken I wanted it to get well on its way. I was confident that Englhardt hadn't seen me at the street corner, but if I passed him now on the highway I'd still have to explain why I took the long, roundabout route from Lucerne to Interlaken.

I found the café beside the lake with no difficulty. It was boarded up for the winter and the lake shore was deserted. I drove down the lane past the clump of trees until I found a place in which to turn around. When I reached the trees again, I pulled in beside them, got out and looked around. I could hear the odd car swishing along the highway but couldn't see it. I unlocked the trunk and lifted the lid a few inches. The ground was soggy so I climbed back into the car and unwrapped the sandwiches. It was a few minutes after one.

An hour later my nerves were beginning to twitch so I got out of the car and walked along the lane until I could see the highway. The morning mists had long since disappeared and the sun was hot and strong. A crisp breeze ruffled the surface of the lake tipping the wavelets with silver, and I wished I'd thought to borrow a fishing rod from the hotel. Beyond the valley, the Jungfrau was sporting a sombrero of cotton wool.

I heard the sound of a car decelerating and glanced towards the café in time to see the Sunbeam swing into the lane, scattering gravel. At the shore it turned and backed up until it was abreast of the Buick. Englhardt jumped out, gave me a broad smile and unlocked the trunk. I flipped up the back lid of the Buick.

"I am sorry I am late," he said, heaving out a small canvas sack. I took it and almost dropped it. The weight for its size was incredible. "That *verdampt* woman couldn't make up her mind about a place for the picnic."

"I was beginning to worry." With no little effort I got the sack into the trunk. "Everything all right?"

He handed me another sack. "Perfect. But it was a long night's work."

"You'll be able to sleep well tonight. Your friend, too, now that this stuff is out of his house."

"He said the same thing."

For the next few minutes we were silent as we transferred the sacks from one car to the other. There were about fifteen of them and I guessed their weight at something like forty pounds each. I had had no idea that platinum for its size was that heavy. The back of the Buick was beginning to sag and I decided to distribute some of the weight forward after Englhardt had departed.

Finally all the platinum was moved, and he tipped back his hat and mopped his brow. I was feeling the strain myself —shifting more than six hundred pounds of dead weight in under two minutes had brought into play muscles I didn't even know I owned.

He climbed in behind the wheel of his car. "I'm sorry we cannot go and have a drink to celebrate this moment," he said with considerable feeling. "I have been looking forward to it for over a year."

"Well, I'll be celebrating tomorrow night—when this stuff is stored in the vaults of the bank."

He engaged the gear. "Are you returning via Bern?"

"No—ah, no. I'll be going straight to Lucerne."

"Yes, I should," he said, showing his powerful teeth in a quick grin. "It's never amusing to retrace one's steps." And then with a "Good luck!" he drove rapidly down the lane.

I stood there like a guilty schoolboy. How in the hell had he found out I'd been to Bern?

CHAPTER THREE

TWO WEEKS PASSED before I saw Englhardt again. But I heard from him practically every other day and I began to think that he had nothing better to do than sit in his office composing long, discursive letters to me on everything from the Russian ballet to the American reaction should Soslov replace Khrushchev. He wrote by hand in a large flowing script and although his English was stilted, it was fluent. His knowledge of the current European cultural scene was considerable.

And in nearly every letter, sandwiched somewhere between Gide and Shostakovich, would be the name and address of an individual in Milan or London or Stockholm to whom I could sell another ten, fifteen or twenty kilos of platinum. As a result, during those two weeks I traced a spiderweb of trails across Western Europe and, since all transactions were on a cash and carry basis, the center of the web became Lausanne. On one or two occasions I was sorely tempted to save time and shove a few kilos in my suitcase, but a bit of rational thinking made me appreciate that the reputation of the Transeastern Supply Company would not be enhanced if its director were called up on a smuggling charge.

Gradually the safe deposit boxes emptied; in the fortnight I got rid of 155 kilos and had deposited nearly $300,000 in each of the two bank accounts Englhardt had indicated. Both these accounts were under numbers and only the director of the bank knew the name of the holder. It was an old Swiss custom in which a person could operate a bank account with complete anonymity. Even the police could not obtain the owner's name.

It was a cold, rainy Sunday morning. I had planned to spend it in my apartment catching up on my own affairs when Englhardt telephoned and said he was in Paris and would like to have lunch with me. I accepted and he asked me to meet him at Var, a White Russian restaurant off the Champs Elysées.

He greeted me with a wonderful smile, threw his arm around my shoulders and squeezed my hand in his ham-like fist. And I soon found the liverish morosity with which I'd awakened quickly dissipating in the warmth of his personality. He served me himself from the enormous table of *zakuski;* then followed at his command *blinis* and caviar, *shashlik karsky* roasted in front of an open fire and I knew I'd eat no more that day. We washed it down with Polish vodka and, although he didn't smoke, he insisted on selecting for me the most expensive cigar the house offered.

And it was not until the coffee was served that he evinced the slightest interest in the platinum or my activities since he'd left me standing, embarrassed, beside the Swiss lake. Then it was only to inquire how many kilos I'd sold. I gave him a slip of paper on which I'd noted the quantity sold, the expenses and the amounts I'd deposited in the two accounts. He gave it a casual glance and handed it back to me.

"Good," he said. "Now we must begin the second and more interesting phase."

I threw him a wry look and remembered the planes, the hotels and the hanging around strange offices and the bickering with their even more strange occupants during the past days. At least, I thought, the fact that he was $300,000 richer should call forth a more dramatic comment than just "good." For the first time I began to wonder if money, as such, had any real meaning for Nicholas Englhardt.

"To begin with," he went on, "I thought we should form a company in Luxembourg. But now—"

"I have a company," I pointed out. "Why not use it as our outlet and save time? It can easily be arranged for you to receive your percentage of the profits."

"Your company is incorporated in the United States, is it not?"

"Yes."

"Then it is of no use. It is not in my area. I can only authorize the sale of merchandise to firms in Belgium or Luxembourg. American companies are dealt with through our commercial department in Washington."

"I see. Then it had better be Luxembourg. The taxes are less."

"Exactly. But instead of forming a company, it will be better if we buy one. I have the names of three or four export companies which can be acquired for very little. By using an established firm, I won't have to explain why I'm dealing with a newly formed concern."

"A good point."

He got out his enormous wallet and after some search found a card. "Here is the name of a firm of lawyers in Luxembourg, and here—" he turned the card over "—are the names of three small companies, each of which I know the directors will sell for around $20,000. You can probably get one of them for considerably less. However, I would sooner you paid what they ask. I do not like parsimonious dealings. Now you go and see these lawyers on Monday. They know—"

"Just a minute!" I smiled and held up a protesting hand. "I'm afraid there are a few of my own affairs I must give attention to. You see, for the past fortnight—"

"I am sorry!" he broke in, his solicitous eyes searching mine. "But you should have told me! Of course you must look after your own business first. And you must tell me if I can be of any help."

His voice was so apologetic, I hastened to explain that my agent in Cairo had asked me to come out because he was having trouble renewing a large contract with an Egyptian cotton firm.

"We are finding Russian competition pretty keen these days," I said. "What are you trying to do, drive us out of the eastern markets?"

"At least we are selling our products. Under the Marshall Plan and ECA, your government gave them away."

The illogicality of this man's thinking was again brought home to me. A moment ago he had been ingeniously planning how he could personally benefit from his country's new policy of underpricing competition out of world markets. And yet when I complain about that same unfair trade war, immediately his hackles rise. Was it because I was an American criticizing the Russians?

"Is there much difference," I argued, "between selling for one percent down and the rest of your life to pay and a free gift? At least the gift doesn't require any bookkeeping."

"Depends, Mr. Sherman, on how many strings are attached to the gift."

"Am I to presume that there are no Marxist tracts attached to your bargain sales slips?"

Englhardt sat back and laughed. "Perhaps so, Mr. Sherman. But as that *schouft* Shepilov found out when he last visited Egypt, those Arab beggars can't read. They only know how to put their hand in our pocket—or yours."

"In the meantime, I am quietly being squeezed out of business."

His expression was suddenly full of concern. "So long as I can help you, Mr. Sherman, you will never be squeezed out of business."

For a long moment I stared at him. "You know, Englhardt," I said slowly, "I have a feeling you mean that."

The following Tuesday afternoon I landed in Cairo and my agent, Jack Brent, met me at the airport with a face as long as his necktie. During the drive into the city he informed me that a contract we had had with the Al Ahram Cotton Mills for the past eight years had not been renewed, and that if things continued as they were going, we might as well close up the office. With Englhardt as my ace in the hole, I obviously was not as depressed with the situation in Egypt as I should have been. I told him to relax, that the world was a big market. Besides, if the Russians could produce the goods, maybe we had better start doing business with them. The look he gave me was one of considerable horror.

On Wednesday morning I called the director in charge of purchasing for the Al Ahram Cotton Mills and invited him to lunch. I waited until after the main course to ask him why he hadn't renewed our contract. I suggested that since I knew our machinery was the best on the market, perhaps the price wasn't right.

"I explained everything to Mr. Brent," he said, rather plaintively.

"Yes, he told me. But I want to hear you explain it to me." He lowered his head and threw out his hands in a typical Arabian gesture. He probably had been selling brass ashtrays to tourists in some cluttered bazaar before Nasser cleaned out the big-time grafters ; then men like my lunch guest had pulled themselves out of the *soulks* by the army's coattails.

"Okay," I went on when he said nothing, "what is it? Are you looking for another raise in your pay-off?"

"Oh, no, Mr. Sherman." And if there were no tears in his eyes, there were in his voice. "You must understand; you only lose one contract, but I lose the commission and I have a large family to support."

"You're going to find it tough living on your salary." I had no sympathy for him. He had squeezed every dollar out of me and I knew he had been doing the same with the other foreign firms his company dealt with.

"Yes, Mr. Sherman, you don't have to remind me. But the government has taken it out of our hands. They will no longer give us an import license unless we purchase our equipment from the suppliers they designate."

"In other words, the Russians. I wasn't aware that they could manufacture cotton processing machinery that would hold a candle to what we supply."

"They are not, but the Czechs are."

That afternoon I called on an official I'd been friendly with in the commercial department of the Egyptian Government. I asked him frankly if they were trying to squeeze Western companies out of Egypt. He was prepared for the question; obviously, I was not the first exasperated foreigner to knock on his door. He brought out a thick file and turned up the contract which had been refused. Attached to it was a sheet of paper containing the prices for comparable Czech machinery. They were at least fifty percent lower.

"Those are dumping prices," I said, "and you know it. Even with the use of sweated or forced labor it is not possible to manufacture that machinery at those prices."

He shrugged and lifted his hands. "We are not interested in the economic or political reasons for their offering us the machines at these prices. We are a neutral country and if your firm can meet the price, we will of course continue to do business with you."

I got up. "Send me a postcard when the commissar takes over your office," I said rather bitterly.

The last call I made was on the commercial attaché of the United States Embassy. He was most sympathetic, but suggested I try a higher level in Washington.

"Any use?" I asked him.

"Quite frankly, I don't think so," he was honest enough to admit. "The Russians have us over a barrel. Whatever price you quote, they'll cut in half. And if you give it away they'll give away double."

"One more question—I have an international supply company, as you know. What's wrong if I cut in on some of this Russian trade?"

"Nothing, provided you don't deal in anything on the strategic list."

"Seems to be shrinking every day."

"You fellows have to live."

I returned to the Transeastern office and asked Brent how long since he'd been on the road. He looked at me in blank amazement for a moment, took off his glasses and slowly polished them with his handkerchief.

"You mean, selling?"

"Exactly," I said. "Door to door."

"Well, Mr. Sherman, I've been your manager here for almost six years. And before that—"

I smiled. "But you haven't forgotten how to sell?"

He put his glasses back on, carefully tucked the handkerchief into his breast pocket and rather weakly returned my smile. "I don't think so. This is a selling job basically, only on a much higher level."

"Good. Tomorrow morning I want you to start closing this office. Don't give up the lease; we might need the space later on. Ship any files you think worth keeping to New York, store the office equipment and come to Paris when you're through. I have another job for you."

Brent gulped a couple of times, and as the color drained out of his face I realized that I might have swung the axe with a little more tact. But his first question proved to me that I had a good man working for me.

"What will I do about the staff?" he asked.

"Let's see, you've got the secretary, Miss Maudet; the stenographer—I've forgotten her last name—and the office boy, Abdul. Give the stenographer and Abdul three months' salary in lieu of notice and explain that their new government has put us out of business. As for Miss Maudet, I hate to lose sight of her. She's always struck me as being a very smart girl."

"Yes, she is very efficient."

"Have you a file on her? A dossier or whatever you keep on your employees?"

Brent pulled open a drawer and after some search came up with a typewritten sheet of paper. "Only the bare details, I'm afraid."

I looked it over. "French citizen," I read aloud. "Age twenty-two, which means she's twenty-six now. Born Shanghai, French father and—oh my God! Russian mother!" I laughed. "These Russians are certainly getting into my hair! Sorbonne, etc., and etc. Speaks French, English, German and Russian." I glanced up at Brent. "Sure you've been paying her enough? This gal's got qualifications."

Brent smiled, a little smugly I thought. "I discovered her in Nice. She was working in a travel agency."

I tossed him a quizzical look. "Have you any, ah, interest other than commercial in her?"

"Certainly not, Mr. Sherman!" he said, unable to control the blush that started up from his collar.

"Okay, okay, but you've got to admit she's a damned good looking girl. If I'd been stuck out here like you, I don't know if I would have been so disinterested."

"I'm sure Miss Maudet has her own private life outside this office," he observed rather stiffly.

"Something wrong with the local boys if she hasn't. I'll sound her out and see if she would like to work for us in Luxembourg."

"Luxembourg, Mr. Sherman?" I could see his ears pricking. "And what would the type of work involve?"

"Same thing she's doing here in a different language."

I walked out of Brent's office and stopped by Miss Maudet's desk. "You're working overtime," I said. "Does that slave driver in there always keep you this late?"

"Oh, no," she protested primly. "But I felt that since you were still here I would remain in case you needed me."

While we were talking, my eyes ran over her figure. She was well built with plenty of curves in the right places. And her hair, the texture of silk and the color of sunlight on golden-ripe wheat, must have driven the Arabs crazy. Her eyes were tawny, level and not shy and her mouth was soft with a touch of firmness which suggested that those lips didn't kiss often but when they did there'd be no nonsense about it. She was wearing a plain white cotton dress that despite a sweltering day in the office looked crisply fresh.

And suddenly I decided to break a long-standing rule about never casting a personal eye on the female staff. At the time I excused it by thinking that I should find out more about this young woman before bringing her to Luxembourg to work in the new company. If I'd been completely honest, I would also have had to admit that I was bored with the prospect of spending an evening in Cairo alone or in Brent's not too stimulating company.

At any rate, I asked her to have dinner with me.

"Thank you," she said without change of expression—no surprise, no particular pleasure, just a polite "Thank you" and I began to wish I'd remained in my place. "I will telephone and cancel the plans I'd already made," she continued.

"No, no," I protested. "Perhaps another time—"

"But it is nothing." This time the firm line of her mouth softened and her lips opened in a warm smile.

We went to el Sheradz. I had suggested calling for her, but she said that she would meet me at the restaurant. I'd already had two martinis in the bar when she arrived—I had the impression that although she might toy with a drink, it wasn't one of her favorite pastimes and I don't like forcing people to sit around while I enjoy my pre-dinner quota.

She was wearing a dark green dinner dress which brought out the burnished gold of her hair. It was also designed to accentuate the tiny waist and very full, very curvaceous bosom and I wondered if Brent had gotten her particulars right. She reminded me more of the current mode in Italian movie stars rather than a Franco-Russian combination. When she walked into the bar the eyes of all the unattached men—and several of the attached—swung in her direction. I suppressed a complacent smile and reminded myself that she was only dining with me because I was the boss. And as I lifted her hand to my lips and caught the elusive scent of some exotic perfume, I warned myself to remember that fact.

She ordered dinner carefully and with true Gallic perception, and I asked her to suggest which of the local dishes were interesting. She drank wine with appreciation and it enriched the glow of her complexion. She was a gay companion and laughed easily and until the dusky Arab brought us Turkish coffee, the Transeastern Supply Company to all intents and purposes didn't exist. Brent, I decided, needed no coaching when it came to selecting secretaries. I also understood how he maintained a purely impersonal relationship with Miss Maudet. She was much too attractive to start thinking about during office hours. Or perhaps he had, and had been snubbed. I could believe it. Despite her charming, unaffected personality, I had a suspicion that Miss Maudet's sights were aimed very high.

"Were you speaking with Mr. Brent after I left?" I inquired while lighting her cigarette.

She glanced across at me and like a mask slipped on her office expression of impersonal politeness. "No," she said. "Should I have told him I was having dinner with you?"

"Heavens, no!" I laughed. "He'd probably fire you on grounds of jealousy." I hunched forward in my chair. "No, I was wondering if he had told you that we are closing down the agency here."

"Closing the office?" There was decidedly more than polite interest in her tawny eyes now. "You mean we are going out of business?"

"In Egypt, yes. The rest of the world, certainly not." I explained what we were up against in the Near East and why I considered it useless to continue maintaining an agency here. In her position as Brent's secretary she knew as well as I did how much business we had been losing, but I had the feeling that it rather shocked her to learn I was throwing in the towel so easily. No doubt the assumption that she would be out of a job had some bearing on her reaction.

"I'm starting a new company in Europe—Luxembourg, to be more precise," I explained. "It will be an entirely separate organization from Transeastern and I will need a staff." I paused long enough to tell the waiter to refill the cognac glasses. "Now there are several questions I'd like to ask before I offer you a position."

Slowly, without taking her eyes off me, she stubbed out her cigarette.

"I understand you're not married," I went on. "Have you any family here?"

"No. My mother lives in Paris. My father died during the war. I have two sisters, both of whom are married. One lives in San Francisco, the other in Paris. They're both older." She smiled. "That's all."

"Have you—and you must excuse me for being inquisitive—any roots down here?" I had no desire to pry into her private life. But she was an extremely attractive woman, so it seemed only reasonable to presume that some member of the local foreign colony was carrying a torch for her. And I didn't want to go to the trouble and expense of transferring her to Luxembourg and starting her in with a new company only to have her resign in a couple of months because she was lonesome for the man she'd left behind. "I mean," I explained, "would you be happy returning to Europe?"

"I would love it!" she declared with such vehemence my eyebrows shot up.

I waited a moment for her to enlarge on her statement, but she didn't. "Sounds like you don't like Cairo." I grinned at her. "Any particular reason? Or am I becoming too personal?"

Without answering, she leaned forward and took another cigarette out of the package on the table. I held my lighter across.

"Well, at least I know you're willing to come," I said reflectively, and decided to leave it at that. Obviously she considered her reason or reasons for wishing to leave Egypt none of my damned business. "The second point, and I want you to know this before we go any further, is that I'm setting up this company to do business with the Russians."

"Russians? The Communists?"

"Yes, they're the only ones with money these days. Now, I know your mother was a White Russian, and some of you people have very strong aversions to any sort of dealings with the Reds. Can't say I blame you."

"You mean, you are going to help them?"

With some difficulty I choked back a snort and wished that I could give some indication of just what Englhardt and I were up to. I had the impression that she would have enjoyed it. But it was too dangerous. If I had to lose her services and—I suddenly realized this was much more important—her esteem, then so be it. There could be only two men in the world to know the real reason for the Luxembourg company. Since Englhardt's life depended on his secrecy, I knew he would never talk. And even with Dmitri Smirnoff, I had not gone into details.

"No, Miss Maudet," I said finally. "We are not going to help them. But I'm not letting my ideologies interfere with my intelligence. We cannot build a wall around half the world, and the day is coming—I think it has already arrived—when we must do business with the Iron Curtain countries. Either that," I shrugged, "or be prepared to fight a war of extermination when they decide to break out."

In view of what Englhardt and I had in mind, I felt like a hypocrite expounding these sentiments to her. But at the same time, I was honestly convinced that the more we could infiltrate into the Communist world either through trade, cultural exchange or just plain tourism, the more understanding there would be on both sides and the less chance there would be of that final armageddon.

She leaned back in her chair and laughed. "It is perhaps better I never tell my mother," she said. "Because she would certainly disown me if she knew I was going to work with the Communists."

We were among the last to leave the restaurant, and if she hadn't called my attention to the fact the sleepy waiter was eyeing us with sadness, I probably even then wouldn't have called for the check. Out in the street I suggested that since it was still early she should show me what the local night life had to offer. At first she rather definitely declined, and I felt as though she had sent me back to the front office. But I pointed out that if I didn't show up next day it would be because I'd gotten into trouble wandering around this sinful city alone, and she laughed and said all right, she'd take me to a bistro she knew for a nightcap. It was within walking distance and, as we strolled through the soft African night, I slipped my arm through hers and decided it was possible to mix business with pleasure, after all.

The bistro turned out to be a cabaret with soft music, poor champagne and a check that emptied my purse. But I rolled into bed at four A.M. with the thought that it had been many years since I'd enjoyed myself so thoroughly. Vera Maudet—it was Vera after midnight—dropped me off at my hotel. She had been very definite in her refusal to allow me to take her home in the taxi and it finally dawned on me that perhaps she was a little worried about my intentions. Since I wasn't too sure of them myself, I said goodnight outside the hotel and made some stupid observation about fixing things with Brent if she were late for work that day.

After a lengthy lunch with an old business acquaintance I went to the office to ask Brent about planes to Paris. I had nothing more to keep me in Cairo and I was suddenly anxious to get going with the Luxembourg company. There was crushed ice in the looks I got from both the office boy and the stenographer and I assumed Brent had lowered the axe. The greeting I received from Vera as I crossed her office was hardly less formal if not so cold, and I found it slightly disconcerting to think that less than a dozen hours ago I was holding her sultry body close to mine while we swayed to soft music. Despite the intense heat, she was wearing a scarf of some filmy material around her neck, and I sincerely hoped Brent hadn't noticed the heavy circles under her eyes. Or at least that he didn't know I was responsible.

Brent explained that it was not going to take as long as he had thought to close the agency, and that with any luck he should be in Paris in one week. I told him to contact me when he arrived.

He asked me what kind of work I had in mind for him, and I told him that he would be on the road most of the time. His salary would remain the same and there would be a commission on his sales. This pleased him so I remarked that I hoped he had no patriotic or other objections about selling Iron Curtain country products. I could see that this question disturbed him, so I hastened to explain that we had been given the green light by our commercial attaché, provided we didn't go into strategic materials. Finally he shrugged and said that since it appeared to be inevitable, we might as well be among the first. I heartily agreed.

The first plane I could catch was an Air France leaving the next morning. It called at Rome and I asked Brent to book me a passage to Paris with a night stop-over in Rome. There were two or three business affairs I had to attend to there and this would give me the opportunity. And after inviting Brent to come and have a drink with me that evening, I left his office.

As I passed Vera's desk, I paused and she buried her face in an open letter file. Her nervous twitch as she drew the scarf tighter drew my attention to it. It was not difficult to see the series of small purplish bruises which circled her neck.

It was obvious that someone had attempted to strangle her.

"I had a wonderful time last night," I said brightly. "In fact, if I'd known you had such a gay town here I'd have come more often."

She glanced up at me now, but the smile she gave me didn't reach her eyes. "It was fun, wasn't it?"

"Have you made up your mind about Luxembourg?"

"I decided that last night. When do you wish me to come?"

"As soon as Mr. Brent can release you. There's going to be a lot of paper work connected with the formation of the new company and I'll certainly need you." I held out my hand. "Well, I'm off in the morning, so I guess this is goodbye for now. See you in Luxembourg." I continued to hold her hand for a moment while I contemplated her. "Look," I said quietly, carefully choosing my words, "I dislike intensely people who pry into other people's personal affairs. So I'll only say this: if you need me, forget I'm the man in the front office and remember I'm your friend."

She withdrew her hand and stared down at her desk and with a touch of panic I was afraid she was going to burst into tears. But when she looked up at me again, her eyes were clear, level and very calm.

"Thank you, Mr. Sherman," she said evenly. "It's very kind of you."

I walked out of her office feeling as though I had gone to attend a friend's funeral only to discover he hadn't died.

The plane left at twelve and with nothing better to do I taxied out to the airport early and checked through the customs and police. I was buying some magazines when the flight departure was called but I caught up to the straggling line of passengers halfway across the tarmac—and practically walked into Vera

Maudet. In one hand she was carrying a dressing case and in the other a portable typewriter.

"Well, hello!" was all I could think of to say as I eased the typewriter out of her hand.

"Mr. Brent decided he wouldn't need me and that perhaps you did," she explained calmly.

"I certainly do!" I admitted with a grin. "And I'm glad you brought this." I lifted the typewriter. "I'll put you to work in Rome."

She was dressed in a smart pearl gray suit and tiny felt hat. Over her arm was slung a camel's hair travelling coat and she looked serene, self-possessed and very beautiful, not at all like a woman who had, in one night, cleared out of a city in which she'd been living for four years. Her eyes were on mine so I studiously avoided staring at the green scarf around her throat.

We had started up the steps when the sound of a commotion behind drew my attention. I glanced over my shoulder and noticed a tall, powerfully built, very dark Arab struggling with a policeman and two or three Air France attendants over by the terminal building. They were all shouting in Arabic of which I understand nothing. Then the man behind me gave me a polite nudge and I moved into the plane.

"Looks like one of your passengers has lost his ticket," I said to the hostess as I showed her mine.

"Just as well," she said with a smile. "We're already full up."

We landed in Rome at five and took a taxi into the city. I got out at the Fiat offices and told Vera to continue on to the Excelsior with the luggage and book two rooms. I said I'd be there before dinner with some reports for her to type.

I reached the hotel at seven-thirty, entered the room and discovered my suitcase had been unpacked, the clothes hung up, the dressing gown put on the bed; the slippers underneath it. I had stayed at the Excelsior many times before but had never found personal service like this. I stripped down to the waist and was

filling the washbasin when there was a knock on the connecting
door to the bedroom. I called out, and Vera entered.

"You in the next room?" I said over my shoulder.

"Yes. I thought it would be more convenient since you said
you have some work for me to do."

"Excellent. Dig into my briefcase and in the first compartment you'll find some correspondence referring to a shipment
of light trucks from the Fiat factory. Take it with you and give
me a report summarizing the complaints. Oh, and by the way, if
you're responsible for the room service, thanks! You're going to
spoil me."

It took some time to get rid of the Egyptian dust but when
I walked back into the bedroom she was still there, leaning
against the edge of a table, the file of letters in her hand. Her
eyes followed me as I got out a clean shirt and put it on. And
for some peculiar reason—and I'm far from prudish—when I
glanced across and found her staring at me I experienced a powerful physical emotion that disturbed me. It bore no relation to
the amorous and slightly alcoholic desire I'd felt for her that
night in Cairo. I had the feeling that if, instead of putting on
a shirt, I'd stripped everything off, her smoldering eyes would
not have shifted.

With a twinge of guilt, I kicked the thought away, picked up
a tie and reminded myself that I was not accustomed to having
a woman hanging about my room. "Have you had dinner yet?"
I asked.

"No."

"You'd better go and get it. I'm afraid I have another appoint-
ment at nine." I glanced at my watch. "And knowing these
Italians that means dinner. I hope it doesn't mean a night on the
town afterward."

She straightened up. "Do you want this report tonight?" Her
voice and manner were completely impersonal and my guilt
increased.

"Hell, no," I said brusquely. "We'll be here until tomorrow afternoon, and you can do it in the morning." I started towards the door. "By the way, if you need any local currency draw it from the hotel cashier. I'll leave word."

She said thank you very formally and I went out, wishing that I could have apologized to her. But just how one apologizes for one's reprehensible thoughts, I didn't know.

It was long after midnight when I returned to the hotel, feeling very full of pasta, chianti and international trade problems. I let myself into the room and spent a minimum of time getting into bed. I switched off the lamp and discovered the french windows were full of moonlight. Remembering the dawn's early light, I was trying to work up enough energy to get up again and close the curtains when there was a light knock on the door to the adjoining room.

Before I could answer, the door pushed open and Vera came in. She was holding a dark negligee loosely about her and her long hair, like a golden cape in the moonlight, fell about her shoulders.

"I'm terribly sorry to disturb you," she said quietly, "but have you any sleeping pills? I'm afraid the excitement of leaving Cairo has finally caught up with me."

"I was wondering when it would," I said, snapping on the bedside lamp and smiling up at her. "Quite frankly, I don't know how you managed everything so quickly." And then, since I never wear pajamas, I told her I would look in my dressing case and bring her whatever I had.

She returned to her room and I got up and put on my dressing gown. I had no sleeping pills but I did have some Swiss pain killers which I presumed would have a soothing effect on the nerves. I found them, filled a glass with water and went in to her room. She was lying on top of the bed and I sat down beside her and handed her the pills.

"Not sure they'll put you to sleep," I said, "but they should quiet your nerves."

She swallowed one, drank some water and set the glass down on the bedside table. "Did you have a succesful evening?" she asked.

"I can think of other things I'd sooner have been doing," I said, acutely conscious of her golden brown body beneath the almost transparent negligee.

"Such as?" Our eyes met and spoke their own language.

"For one thing," I said softly, putting my arms around her and drawing her close to me, "this." Her lips were soft, moist and the pressure of her warm body against mine set my senses on fire.

Sometime during the night she must have gotten up and closed the curtains, for when I awakened it was nine o'clock and I had to switch on the lamp to see my wristwatch. She was quietly sleeping, her back to me. I turned off the light, crept out of bed and returned to my own room and closed the door.

A large pot of coffee failed to soothe my seething thoughts. I rang for the waiter again and told him to bring me a bottle of whisky. But a drink only made things much worse. I went back to her room and got into bed. She turned towards me and whispered good morning and we made love again.

At noon I told her I had to get up, that there were a few things I should attend to before the plane departed. She asked if they were important, and I gazed down into the tawny eyes full of slumbering passion and said no; nothing was important outside the four walls of this room.

That evening we went out and had dinner and walked slowly back along the Muro Torto in the moonlight. In our rooms I asked her if she would like some champagne. But by the time it had cooled in its ice bucket we were no longer interested in wine.

We got up in time to catch the afternoon plane to Paris. At the airport she was cool, reserved and I was "Mr. Sherman." In the plane she brought out the report I'd asked her to type and proceeded to discuss certain aspects of it with considerable intelligence. I listened for a time but when the plane levelled off and the engines settled down I put my hand over hers and fell asleep.

At Orly I hired a taxi. She said she would be staying with her mother, and I dropped her off outside a gray block of apartments on. the Rue des Longchamps and sent the chauffeur up with her luggage.

"Here is the address and phone number." She handed me a small card. "Let me know when you want me."

She held out her hand and I kissed it. I could find nothing to say but so long. She turned and disappeared into the building.

The following morning, early, I left my apartment, picked up the car and headed for Luxembourg. Unconsciously, I think I wanted to get away before the phone rang. I don't know. When I reached the open highway, I pushed the Mercedes to the limit and roared through the crisp, clean, spring morning as though I were trying to outpace memory.

CHAPTER FOUR

I THREW MYSELF into the complicated business of locating and buying a Luxembourg export company. I finally settled for a small family firm, mainly because I liked the director. He was a delightful antiquarian with a keen and lively interest in life, and I derived a considerable amount of pleasure in knowing that the Communists would be paying for this conservative capitalist's retirement. Next I had to find my own dummy directors who would reassign their stock to me, and register the transfer of ownership with innumerable government agencies. Fortunately the staff presented no problem. It consisted of one ancient, round-shouldered and rheumy character who sat on a high stool and kept his books with a pen, and a middle-aged, mouse-colored stenographer. I sent the old man home and told him to stay there, that I'd send him his salary each month. I could afford to be generous. He was earning less than what I would have had to pay an office boy in New York. I inspected the work of the stenographer and found it excellent despite a typewriter that should have been in the Smithsonian Institute. She said yes, she would like to continue working with the new owners. I doubled her salary and sent her out with tears in her eyes to buy a new typewriter.

The office consisted of three small rooms just off the Avenue de la Liberté. They were musty, dark and full of old furniture, fly-spotted lithographs of clipper ships and memories. I itched to have the place painted. But the integrity of Duchamp, Fils & Cie. would stand up under the scrutiny of Russia's most suspicious trade inspector.

I had written to Englhardt's private address in Brussels and told him I was staying at the Grand Cravat in Luxembourg and once more the flow of letters began. He was bubbling over with enthusiasm and impatient to start work, and said he would meet me at Spa the next Sunday. I found myself eagerly looking forward to seeing him again.

The press of work during the day kept my mind active, but sometimes at night or early in the morning I would wake up sweating with the memory of Rome. And I would ask myself why I didn't send for her. There was a good reason for her to be here. She would be of inestimable help in the office. In fact, I knew that if I waited any longer she would realize when she did come that I'd deliberately postponed asking her.

But should I send for her? Would I be able to work with her physical presence so near? Wouldn't it be safer to explain that the position wasn't big enough for her, and find her a post in some other country? That wouldn't mean I couldn't see her from time to time.

I picked up the telephone and asked for Paris.

"I thought I'd been fired." Her voice was bright with a twist of humor and I knew those brown eyes were smiling.

"The lawyers took longer than I'd expected," I explained. And then I heard myself telling her to come to Luxembourg.

"Where will I find you?"

I gave her the name of the company and asked her to telegraph the time of her train. "I'll have someone meet you," I said.

"Thank you," she said very politely and hung up.

Slowly I put down the receiver. I wished that I could reach out and touch her.

"You've been working too hard," Englhardt said as he put his long arm around my shoulders. "You look terrible."

I laughed. "I'm worn out pushing those Luxembourg burgomasters around. Why did we choose such a place?"

"Ha! But we'll soon have time to play. Come and I will buy you a bottle of champagne and you will tell me what you have been doing."

He led me out to the terrace of the hotel and chose a table in the sun. I opened my briefcase and got out the documents pertaining to the purchase of the Duchamp Company and began to explain the details.

He held up his enormous hand. "Just tell me two things," he said. "Are you satisfied with this Duchamp and Company?"

"Yes. I think we—"

"Excellent. And now, how much money do you want?"

Slowly I pushed the papers back into my briefcase and closed it. "I wish everyone was as easy to do business with as you," I told him.

"But you haven't started to do business with me yet. I have nothing to do with the Duchamp Company."

"I keep forgetting," I said, grinning at him. "Now, for the money. The cost of the company, the lawyers' fees, etc., and etc.—" I was almost afraid to go into details "—will run about $32,000."

"And you'll need operating capital." He brought out his thick wallet, extracted a check and handed it to me. It was for a hundred thousand dollars and drawn in my name. "Is that enough to start with?" he asked.

I put the check away. "I should think so. If we need any more I will supply it."

"No, Mr. Sherman. You supply your time and experience, I will supply the money. If you require any more, ask me." He handed me a letter. "Here you will find all the particulars of the typewriters I told you about. Tomorrow, as the director of Duchamp, you will write to the commercial attaché of the USSR Embassy in Brussels explaining that you are interested in purchasing these machines and asking for prices and deliveries." He picked up his glass of champagne and drained it.

"And now let us forget these *verdampt* business affairs and enjoy ourselves."

The typewriter deal—I still think of the three enterprises Englhardt and I undertook as the typewriter deal, the camera deal and the motor deal—went through exactly and as smoothly as he had forecast.

Through the auspices of the USSR Ministry of Foreign Trade, the Duchamp Company purchased 24,000 typewriters from an East German manufacturer for 1550 Belgian francs each, payable in thirty days after delivery to a bonded warehouse in Antwerp. How Englhardt arranged this sale without Duchamp having to post a bond I'll never know. Later, he sent me the names of two companies who were interested in buying the machines. One, a Swiss exporting firm, took 10,000 at 2500 francs each; the other, an Anglo-Indian supply house, bought another 3000 at about the same price. I sent Brent off with a few samples to South America by air to get rid of the remainder. Despite the fact he had to bring the price down to compete with Italian and West German dumping prices, we netted a quarter of a million dollars.

The camera deal was, if possible, even simpler. It consisted of 18,000, 35mm cameras of a type similar to the well-known Leica, and made in East Germany. I was to offer 1250 Belgium francs each for them, Englhardt instructed me, and resell them for 2000 francs. But when I received the samples I knew that this camera would retail for three times that sum. I wrote Englhardt accordingly and explained that it was ridiculous for us to put them on the market at the price he had stated. He sent me a very amusing six-page letter in reply, quoting excerpts from the Bible, the classics and Ilya Ehrenburg pointing out the folly of greediness.

And then in a short footnote, he explained that the success of these enterprises depended upon ready capital and even if it meant smaller profits we had to make quick turnovers.

I only saw him once during this period. That was when he came to Luxembourg ostensibly to investigate the Duchamp Company on behalf of his government. After calling on our bankers, he walked into the office and asked to see the director. He had warned me of the visit and I was waiting for him, but when Vera ushered him in, he introduced himself as though we had never met before. Even after she had gone out and closed the door, he continued to play the role without so much as a twinkle in his eye and I decided that the Russian stage had lost a great actor when Nicholas Englhardt chose a commercial career.

We discussed various trade problems and for once he was extremely businesslike and evinced a keen interest in world markets and particularly the American reaction to the Russian export drive. I found myself thoroughly enjoying this new facet of his character.

"We must try to appreciate," he said, "that the world is large enough to provide outlets for both our countries. There is no need for a trade war."

I related my experience in Egypt and suggested that if that wasn't a trade war I didn't know one when I saw one.

"You don't understand," he retorted, his voice booming. "We are forced to use—what do you call it?—the shoehorn. Once we are established in foreign markets, we will bring our prices up to competitive levels and then it will be quality and service which counts."

I threw him a quizzical look. "That's a day I long to see," I said. "But I'm afraid your present leaders will never take politics out of business."

"Perhaps your country should lead the way. You might find the Russians only too willing to follow—we are not afraid of competition. You must remember we are no longer a nation of peasants, slave labor and factories run by political commissars. Come, Mr. Sherman, Russia today is becoming a highly organized, industrial country. In fifty years, provided some *schouft* on one side or the other doesn't drop an H bomb, we will become the most powerful nation on earth."

As I listened to him, I began to wonder if he suspected there was a hidden microphone in the office. Because surely, this sudden bit of flag-waving was not for my benefit. But he appeared perfectly relaxed, completely at ease and no matter how good an actor he might be, I doubt if he would have been able to sit there so obviously enjoying himself if he suspected for one second that his words were being recorded. Moreover, and this amazed me more than anything else, his voice, and the intense, almost fanatical look in his eyes, were completely sincere.

And then, just as I was loading my verbal guns to let go a broadside against the philosophy, freedoms and workers' conditions in a police state, he glanced at his watch, heaved his big frame out of the chair and said that he must go, that his train back to Brussels left in half an hour. Politely, he declined my offer to accompany him to the station, which annoyed me. I wanted to see if, once outside the office, he would drop this role he was playing. And if he did, I fully intended to ask him why, if he was so certain of Russia's future, he jeopardized his own participation in this Soviet Utopia by using his official position to sell his country short. It would have been an interesting answer, and I felt I knew him well enough now to pose the question.

He called out a cheery goodbye to Vera and Miss Gaudin, the stenographer, gave them each a big smile and left.

"Is he really a Communist?" Vera asked with a touch of awe in her voice.

"Well, he works for the USSR Ministry of Trade," I replied, suddenly on my guard. "So I presume he must be one. Why?"

"But he seems so friendly, so natural."

I laughed with relief. "What do you expect these Reds to look like? Two-tailed demons with drooling fangs? It's not what you can see with these boys; they're built like everyone else. It's what's in their minds you've got to worry about."

"He's certainly built!" she exclaimed, her eyes bright "He makes you look small by comparison."

"If you're so interested," I said caustically, "I'll try to fix it for him to take you out the next time he comes."

She threw me a flat look and turned back to her work.

For the first week Vera had been in Luxembourg, there had not been a purely personal word spoken by either of us. She had immediately fitted into the office, made a point of winning over Miss Gaudin and took over completely the work I'd been doing to organize the company along modern lines. More and more I let her manage things and when Brent finally turned up, I whistled him out to the nearest bar and diplomatically explained that I didn't want him wasting his time running a small office that any smart secretary could run, that he was the only salesman and the success of the whole organization rested solely on his shoulders. I moved another desk into my office and told him he could work from there when he wasn't on the road.

Like many Continental offices, we didn't open on Saturdays, and when the first Friday came around, Vera asked me if she could leave an hour early to catch the express to Paris. I said of course, but for some reason I couldn't explain, I didn't tell her that I was driving to Paris myself that evening.

This was about three o'clock. And by four, after watching the hands of the clock move interminably slowly, I gave up trying to suppress the smoldering thoughts that were tormenting me, and told myself I was being a complete damn fool. She would find out I had gone to Paris and she would know then that I was afraid of her. I pushed the buzzer.

"I was driving to Paris in the morning," I lied, "but if you'd care to wait until about eight o'clock, I see now that I can get away tonight."

"That would be wonderful." There was the right amount of polite enthusiasm in her voice but no more, and I immediately regretted my invitation. It was only too obvious that as far as she was concerned, the fire that had blazed up in Rome had long since burned out. "But are you sure you have room?" she asked.

"It's a two-seater, but there'll only be the two of us."

"My suitcase is very small."

"Good. Where'll you be about seven-thirty or eight?"

She gave me the address of the apartment she had taken and I said I'd pick her up there.

The office closed at five-thirty and from then until eight o'clock I sat in the bar of the Continental drinking very dry martinis. By the time I pulled up in front of her apartment house, I had sufficiently anesthetized my emotions, I thought, so that I could drive her to Marseilles if necessary without as much as touching her hand—or wanting to.

"What fun!" she said, climbing in beside me.

"Mind the top down?"

"Oh, no! It's such a beautiful evening!" I watched her as she got out a green scarf and wound it about her head and decided that the trip wasn't going to be as complicated as I'd feared.

We crossed the frontier at Longwy and at Longuyon, and at Verdun I suggested dinner. She said yes, she was famished, so we stopped at the Bellevue. By the time we'd reached the cognac it was almost eleven o'clock.

"You look very tired," she said, her voice full of concern. "Do you want to push on tonight, or stay here and get an early start in the morning?"

"Yes, I am tired," I admitted. But I didn't explain that it was because the martinis had worn off and what I wished to do most in this world was to go to sleep in her arms. Why I didn't tell her, I don't know. Nor did I know why I was fighting her, afraid of her. Because she was my secretary and the situation was impossible? Nonsense. If only that was the case, I reminded myself, I could fire her—and ask her to be my mistress. Or I could ask her to marry me. But would I ever forget the bruised neck in Cairo? Or stop thinking of the tormented devil who had done it?

I went over to the desk, arranged for two rooms and told them to put the car in the garage. I followed her up the stairs and when she paused outside her door, I wanted to say good night but my throat was dry. She asked if I would like to come in for a moment, and then I saw the passion smoldering in those tawny eyes. I nodded.

We never got to Paris that weekend. Saturday, sometime around noon, we left Verdun and drove slowly up to Haybessur-Meuse to a little inn I knew buried in the Ardennes Forest. We were the only guests and since it rained on Sunday, we needed no excuse for not getting up.

On Monday morning, after some reckless driving, I dropped her off at the office only a few minutes late, and returned to my hotel to get some clean clothes. And I had no more idea of what to do about Vera Maudet than I'd had on Friday.

CHAPTER FIVE

FROM THE BEGINNING, I was not too happy about the motors Englhardt had instructed me to buy. Unlike the typewriters or the cameras, they hadn't sent samples. Englhardt had simply explained they were fractional horsepower electric motors and told me what price to offer. I knew there was a big demand for this type of motor in countries like Spain, North Africa and certain parts of the Middle East where water supply was limited and electricity had preceded the development of modern water pressure distribution. And when I first discussed the matter with Brent, he was very enthusiastic and said that he would have no trouble in selling them.

However, when the official specifications arrived from the USSR Embassy and we discovered the motors were of Russian manufacture, Brent lost most of his enthusiasm, and my original fears that this might turn into a commercial fiasco increased. If they had been of East German or Czechoslovakian make, I would not have worried. But Russian! My experience had shown that Russian-made electric motors of small horsepower were too heavy, poorly designed and not reliable. Moreover, for political reasons, it would be impossible to sell Russian goods in Spain.

But—and I couldn't of course discuss this problem with Brent—what excuse was I going to give Englhardt for not carrying out his instructions? If he thought this was going to be a profitable enterprise, the only thing I could do was write to his private address and present my reasons for not being in favor.

And somehow, in view of his recently expressed admiration for new Soviet industrial accomplishments, I was not very certain he would listen to me.

He didn't. In fact he was much more enthusiastic about this deal than the other two. And as far as Spain or any other country which might balk at accepting Russian-made goods was concerned, he said that we would remove the maker's name from the motors and procure a false certificate of origin. He certainly knew all the tricks of the trade.

As a result, Duchamp purchased 30,000 of these motors and I hoped for the best.

By this time, under Vera's guidance in the office and Brent's activities on the road, the company was running along smoothly and I was able to spend more and more time in other parts of Europe looking after Transeastern's affairs.

Returning from one of these trips, Vera informed me that I had just missed Englhardt. He had dropped in late the previous afternoon on his way from Switzerland to Brussels and was very disappointed, she said, that he hadn't seen me.

"Anything particular on his mind?" I asked with considerable apprehension. I was never without a tiny, nagging fear that one day Englhardt would stretch his luck too far.

"No. At least, he didn't say anything. He just wanted to know how things were going."

"You could have told him that."

"I did, in a very general way. And then he invited me out for dinner, and he seemed so lonesome, I thought I'd better be friendly and accept."

"I'm glad you did. We've got to be nice to these people whether we like them or not. And how did you get along with a Communist?"

"He was charming, simply charming!" she said, her eyes sparkling. "And so attractive. I can't believe he's a Red."

I leaned back in my chair and felt a sharp prick of jealousy. "He's charming, all right. And you two would have a lot in common provided you kept off politics."

"Oh, he never mentioned it, nor business either once we had left the office."

That's Englhardt, I said to myself. And then I was about to ask her if he had stayed the night. But I didn't. I was suddenly afraid of her answer. Because if he had, and he'd stayed with her, I know she would have said so.

For the rest of that morning I tried to concentrate on my work, but by one o'clock I knew it was no use. When I was away from Luxembourg and away from her, I found it not difficult to keep my mind on other things. In fact it had reached the point where I jumped at any excuse to leave. And yet, when I had to return, the plane or car couldn't travel fast enough to get me there.

So I spent the early afternoon in the Continental bar, and it was not until four o'clock that I remembered the next day was Saturday and rushed back to the office. She was still there. I gave myself fifteen minutes, and pushed the buzzer.

"Are you going to Paris this weekend?" I asked.

"I hadn't planned to. Is there some work you would like me to do?"

"No—no," I said hesitatingly. And then, "It's so damn hot I thought perhaps we might drive over to Bavaria. It should be cooler in the forest."

"Oh, that would be fun!" she said, her eyes lighting up. "When would you like to leave?"

"Why not this evening—if you're free?"

"Splendid!"

We got away early and spent the first night in a small *gasthaus* outside Schiltach in the Black Forest. I didn't bother with the pretense of taking two rooms, and when the broad-beamed *frau* deposited our luggage in the same room, Vera nonchalantly opened the suitcases and began hanging up the clothes. I went down to the bar and had a drink and a few minutes later she joined me and we ate a delicious if belated *wiernerschnitzel*.

The next day we discovered the view of the valley from the balcony and decided to stay. And late Saturday night, I asked her how it was that she, a White Russian, had got on so well with Englhardt, a Soviet official.

"What you really want to know," she said, rolling over on her stomach and gazing mischievously down at me, "is whether I slept with him. The answer, my sweet, is no."

"You mean he didn't ask you?"

"Quite frankly, we never got around to discussing it."

On Sunday morning we went for a long walk in the forest, ate an enormous lunch and slept most of the afternoon. I got up in time to watch the sun, a red ball of fire, dip below the black ridge of trees. Vera was lying on the bed with only the deepening shadows covering her and with her hair, like molten gold, cascading across the pillows.

"Will you marry me?" I asked her.

"Do you really want me to, Philip?"

"We can't go on like this—it's madness." I sat down beside her.

"Do you love me?"

"Yes—yes, of course I do. I must. I think of you all the time."

"Think of me? Or of my body?"

"What's the difference? It's all you, isn't it?"

She laughed softly and with a sensual, feline movement arched her back and stretched her arms over her head. "In some ways you're very young, Philip." I started to protest, but she went on. "Physically, you're infatuated with me. But you should know that it doesn't always last. And then what?"

"But I love you for more than that."

"What for, Philip? My brains? You already have them—for a hundred and fifty dollars a week. My companionship? No, I don't think so. You are always very careful to live your own life apart from me, week after week, until suddenly you want me and we go away for the weekend."

"And you?" I protested defensively, because somewhere back in my mind I wasn't completely sure she was wrong. "Have you ever considered me as anything more than a bedmate? Or any man?"

She turned towards me and with an impish smile she said, "I must admit you are very satisfactory."

"As satisfactory as that Arab who tried to get on the plane in Cairo?"

"So you noticed him," she said calmly. "He was certainly an experience. But a little too possessive, too violent."

I slid off the bed, poured out a stiff drink, and with jealousy searing my soul like a naked flame, understood how that man felt when he'd put his hands around her throat. I glanced down at mine. They were trembling.

"Does that shock your puritanical sensitivity, Philip?" When I refused to answer, she went on. "You men are all alike. You convince us that you want us, need us, that you can't live without us. So we fall in love with you. And then what happens? We give you everything we have, but eventually you get bored. First it's working late at the office —with the stenographer. Then it's business weekends—with one of your friend's wives. Finally, a sweet young thing comes along and without even bothering with the conventional excuses, you take off after her like a jack rabbit."

She sat up, and with a quick, deft movement tossed her long golden hair back over her shoulders. "Give me a drink, will you?" I handed her a glass. "No, Philip, you see I learned long ago to play the game with your rules. I had to. Life in Europe was not very beautiful in those years after the end of the war. My father was dead and my mother had wasted her time with a man who turned out to be a collaborator. And I was blessed—or cursed— with this body. I was twelve when I discovered the only thing men really wanted." She paused and for a long time gazed out over the darkening valley. "One day I suppose I'll fall in love. And then, no doubt, I'll become the woman of your dreams: placid and faithful and finally boring." She turned her head and looked directly at me. "But now I take what I want when it pleases me."

"And what happens when you don't get what pleases you?"

Her chuckle was throaty. "If you're referring to men, I haven't any idea—it's never happened."

"I can only hope that it happens soon." My eyes dropped away from hers, my thoughts a twisting tangle of emotions in which pity struggled with revulsion while jealousy refereed.

"Why do you dislike me, Philip? A moment ago you asked me to marry you."

"I don't know. I guess I resent this hold you have over me. Or maybe it's your past. Maybe I resent being the latest addition to a long line of vari-colored lovers."

"You do torture yourself, don't you? Why don't you take me as I am? Forget about the past—and the future too, if you like. I work for you, and I enjoy it. I sleep with you and I enjoy that, too. Why don't you leave it at that?"

"No!" I glared down at her. "You have the misfortune—unless you don't think it is—of being able to make a man insanely jealous. And if we go on like this, I'm afraid that one day I'll kill you."

"But why?" Tiny wrinkles creased her smooth brow. "We are both completely free. I don't tell you not to look at another woman. I have no right."

"And you wouldn't care?"

"If you wanted her," she shrugged, "it would mean that you are tired of me. So what can I do about it?"

"You place everything on such a physical basis."

"And you? If I left you now and you knew it wasn't for another man would you still have the same violent reaction?"

"You'd be alone about one week," I retorted.

She laughed softly, and again there was that impish look in her eyes. "Come and sit down."

"No. This argument is ridiculous." I ran my hands through my hair. "Let's get dressed and get the hell out of here."

"As you wish," she said quietly.

I wanted to talk to Brent but rather than wait for him to come in, I left for Paris on Monday and told Vera to have him telephone me there. He did—from Casablanca with a tale of woe about the electric motors. Despite their modern appearance, he said, the damned things were of an old-fashioned type and burned out with any kind of a load. He was beginning to think he couldn't even give them away. I told him to reduce the price and keep trying.

I wrote a long report to Englhardt, passing on Brent's observations and adding a few of my own. I pointed out that if his goal was still ten million dollars, he'd better make an arrangement with his government to take back at least some of the motors on the grounds that they were defective. Because if we got stuck with the lot, we'd not only lose what we made on the first two deals, but he'd have to refinance the company. Although I was itching to do so, I didn't add any comments about the quality of Russian export goods and the reaction of the world market.

A few days later I received an extremely impersonal, almost official note from him implying that there was nothing wrong with the motors, and that he would come to Luxembourg the following day, Friday, to discuss the matter with me. Immediately I sent him a wire, asking him to make it Monday as I had a very important client arriving Friday afternoon from New York.

On Saturday I drove to Luxembourg and went directly to the office in the hope that if Englhardt had not received my message, he would still be waiting in the city. I found a note on my desk from Vera explaining that he had arrived, and that he would return Monday morning. I telephoned her apartment to find out if she knew whether he was staying in Luxembourg for the weekend, but there was no answer.

I telephoned again that evening, and again at midnight. There was still no reply and I tried to go to sleep with the thought that she had, as usual, gone to Paris to see her mother.

I was up with the dawn and cooled my heels until eight o'clock when I drove around to Vera's apartment and asked the concierge if Miss Maudet had gone away for the weekend. The old woman knew me and said yes, that she had gone to Spa.

I think if it hadn't been Sunday morning and all the shops were closed, I would have bought a gun. I don't know. Anyway, the next rational thought I had was when I realized I was in Spa and approaching the Grand Britannique, Englhardt's favorite hotel. I stopped in front of a small café, went in and telephoned the Grand Britannique. I asked if Monsieur Englhardt was registered there. The switchboard girl said he was in Room 411. I said thank you, and hung up. I had a drink and forced myself to take it slowly. I went back to the telephone, called the hotel again and asked if Mademoiselle Maudet had arrived yet. A moment later, she said Mademoiselle Maudet had arrived Friday evening and did I wish to speak with her. I said no, I would come around and see her and asked the room number. The girl said 412, and I mumbled my thanks and hung up.

CHAPTER SIX

I DROVE BACK to Paris and caught the first available plane to New York and for the next two weeks buried myself in the activities of Transeastern. For once, I was glad to find a stack of work waiting for me at the head office.

The days slipped by and as I was no longer under the domination of Englhardt's powerful personality nor distracted by Vera's demoralizing influence—and body—Duchamp and Company began coming into true perspective. And I soon decided that as far as I was concerned it could fold on the spot. It had been a crooked deal to start with, I reminded myself, and it was only poetic justice that we had walked into a beautifully baited Russian bear trap. Because now that I could contemplate with some intelligence the whole fantastic picture, the painful conclusion was that the Reds, with Englhardt's help, had dumped over a million dollars' worth of useless electrical junk on us. Junk which we had paid for with hard currency, and willingly.

At first, I gave Englhardt the benefit of the doubt. His patriotic pride in all things Russian might easily have blinded him to the quality of those motors. But when I considered the facts further—and my resentment toward him for running off with Vera encouraged my suspicions—I began to question his whole story. The platinum for a time stumped me. But a few minutes' calculation convinced me that it had been the bait. And how beautifully he had planted it. Secret conferences! Split-second rendezvous beside deserted lakes! Secret Swiss bank accounts! He'd even been smart enough to explain why the platinum had come from the Bern Embassy. He knew I'd never find out whether it had been hidden in the wall—or in the official safe.

The more I thought about it, the more the pieces fell into place. True, I received my ten percent. But when I added up the time plus the expenses I would have to meet in winding up Duchamp, I didn't consider myself overpaid. Englhardt, I finally decided, was one of the smartest, shrewdest, most likeable operators I'd ever met. And I'd met quite a few. It was unfortunate that his *verdampt* colleagues, had not had the intelligence to play it as cleverly as he had. Because if they had only kept supplying me with reasonably good equipment, in my greediness I would have gone on distributing it around the world. And what difference to the Soviets if Duchamp made a big profit? They would get half of it back through Englhardt, and my share they could write off as the cost of the shoehorn. And when I considered the markets we were getting them into, it was a cheap shoehorn.

I would have to salvage Brent and take care of Miss Gaudin. As for Vera, I hoped that one day she wouldn't find Englhardt's powerful fingers around her beautiful throat. Because I had learned from bitter experience that he was very thorough in everything he did.

It was almost two weeks to the day I arrived in New York when I received an urgent cable asking me to telephone the Luxembourg office. It was signed by Brent and although I had completely lost interest in the company's affairs, I felt duty-bound to support him until I could wind up the company.

I got through almost immediately and I could tell from his voice that something serious had happened. He said that two men who claimed to be Soviet trade officials from Moscow had called the day before and asked a lot of extremely pertinent questions about the operations of the company. He had stalled them by explaining that only the director who was presently in New York could give them the details they wished.

And last night, someone had broken into the office. As far as he could tell, nothing had been stolen. But it looked as though the records had been carefully scrutinized. I asked him if he had reported the affair to the police, and he said no, not yet, that he had wished to inform me first.

"You think there's any connection between your visitors yesterday and the break-in?" I asked him.

"It seems too coincidental to be anything else," he said. "Besides, what is there to steal outside of a couple of typewriters and a calculating machine?"

"If there is nothing missing, don't report it to the police. Is Vera there?" To my surprise, she was. I certainly thought she would have taken off for Moscow or other points east with Englhardt by now.

Her voice still had the power to reach across four thousand miles and start up disturbing thoughts. But her obvious panic drove any personal reflections out of my mind, and I asked her if she had seen Englhardt recently. She said no, not for two weeks. Which, I knew, would be their weekend in Spa.

"Are there any letters from him? You would recognize his handwriting."

"No, nothing."

"He hasn't phoned?"

"No."

That—I couldn't resist the thought—must have been a very unsuccessful weekend. Her voice brought me back.

"Should I try to get in touch with him?"

"No, not yet. Let me talk to Brent again."

After warning him that under no circumstances was he or Vera to try to communicate with Englhardt, I told him to hold the fort, that I'd catch a plane that night and with any luck should be in Luxembourg the following afternoon. I hung up the receiver wondering why the Communists didn't know when the game was over.

I arrived next evening and found Brent waiting at the airport. He may have checked the connections, or he may have been waiting there all afternoon; I didn't ask. We drove to the office and he showed me how they had discovered the files spread around.

"Obviously," I said, "whoever did it doesn't give a damn that we know. Have your visitors been back again?"

"No."

"You said they were from Moscow. How did you know? Did they have cards, or what?"

"They showed me a letter from the USSR Ministry of Trade explaining who they were."

"Did they leave this letter?"

"No. One of them let me read it, then put it back into his pocket."

"And they asked a lot of questions?"

"At first they were extremely polite. They said they were aware that we had been purchasing goods through the Soviet Embassy in Brussels, and wished to know if we found them satisfactory. I explained that with the exception of the motors, we were more than pleased."

"And what did they have to say about those motors?"

"Not much. They were more anxious to find out who the directors of the company were, how long we'd been in existence, our financial structure and so on."

"Hell, they could have gotten that from the bank or by looking up the public records."

"I thought the same thing. However, I felt that it was up to them to know that. Anyway, I simply explained that it was a private company and if they wished any details they'd have to see you, that I was only the sales manager. I was very polite."

"Go on."

"Then they wanted to know who our other customers were. I began to name some of the firms we'd sold their goods to, but they said no, they were interested in the names of the firms we bought from. I skated around this one by again explaining that they'd have to see you."

"And you believe that since they couldn't pump you they broke in to have a look at the records for themselves."

"Seems obvious. And believe me, they looked hard enough!" Brent said caustically. "Personally, I don't think they were trade officials at all. I think they were a couple of MVD thugs."

"And that, of course," I muttered dryly, "would make things really interesting!"

There was, I told myself, only one man who could solve this situation. And that was Englhardt—if he was still in this part of the world. I picked up the telephone—and put it down again. "I've got to get hold of Englhardt," I explained to Brent. "But for various reasons I don't think it's a good idea to telephone the embassy from Luxembourg. Have you got a car here?"

"Yes."

"Good. You drive to Brussels and at nine o'clock tomorrow morning, start trying to get through to him in the commercial department of the Russian Embassy by telephone, telegram, or whatever other means you can think of. But under no circumstances go into the embassy yourself. You might not get out. If you can contact Englhardt, tell him that it is imperative that he come out and meet you. And if he won't come out, then tell him over the phone a couple of Soviet investigators have been going through our records, and let *him* worry about whether the phone is tapped."

"And if I can't raise him?"

"Call me here before you leave Brussels. And by, the way, how good are you with a car?"

For the first time since I'd arrived, a slight smile lifted the corners of his mouth. "You mean, if I'm tailed, can I lose them?"

"Yes."

"Oh, I think I can handle that all right. I'll make a swing around the country before heading for Belgium."

"That's the idea. How's Vera?"

"She went home at noon. This whole affair seems to have been a terrific shock to her."

"Those two characters probably frightened the life out of her. You must remember she's half White Russian." But I was simply making conversation. Vera Maudet wasn't the type, it seemed to me, to be frightened by any man no matter what his color. So why was she putting on an act?

After Brent had gone, I left the office and went to Vera's apartment.

She opened the door to the chain, made sure it was me and slipped it off. She was holding a loose, very wrinkled dressing gown around her and from the state of her hair she had obviously just got out of bed. There was a pale, pinched expression in her face and deep circles under burning eyes. I began to think that maybe this was no act. But when I noticed the overflowing ashtrays and a half-empty bottle of whisky on the table, I began to wonder if she weren't suffering from the effects of a prolonged binge. Whatever the cause, seeing her stirred up my emotions once again, with pity added to the acid brew of hatred and desire.

"What have you got to eat?" I asked cheerfully.

She pushed the hair back off her forehead and pulled the dressing gown tighter. "There's a steak or some eggs," she said listlessly. "What would you like?"

"Both, with the steak underneath. Have you eaten lately?"

"Well, yes, I suppose so."

I picked up the whisky bottle. "How be you fix up something for both of us while I catch up on my drinking?" I didn't offer to pour her a drink. I wanted her to ask for one. But she didn't. I walked over and put my hand under her chin and lifted her face. Her breath carried a trace of alcohol, but it was very faint.

"What are you doing?" she demanded, brushing my hand away.

"Just checking up," I said, touching her lips with mine. "Now what about that steak?"

She stood there a moment, her tawny eyes widely open, staring at me. Then she turned and disappeared into the bedroom. I poured myself a drink, kicked the footstool over to the couch, sat down and put my feet up.

When she reappeared a few minutes later, my eyebrows shot up in surprise as I caught sight of the alteration not only in her attire but in her expression. She had put on a short, maroon-colored housecoat and black silk slacks and her hair hung in two thick golden braids down to her waist. The worried wrinkles had smoothed out of her face and even the dark circles seemed to have retreated. And that sultry light I knew so well had crept back into her eyes.

She leaned over and picked up my empty glass and as her thigh brushed against my elbow I clenched my fists in my pockets. She poured me another drink and said that supper would be ready in a minute.

Later that evening I said, "When you last saw Englhardt, did you discuss the Duchamp Company with him?"

"You mean, when he came here the last time?"

"I mean when you spent the weekend with him in Spa." But she was too smart—or too indifferent—to give me the satisfaction of reacting to that statement.

"I gathered you'd found out about the weekend," she said casually. "But you shouldn't have run away. I could have used a manly shoulder to cry on."

"What was the matter?" I demanded caustically. "Didn't he have any sleeping pills to bring you?"

Sudden anger flared in her eyes, but her voice was under control as she said, "I guess I deserved that crack."

"Okay," I said, "I'm not interested in the gory details of your amorous adventures. But I am interested in what happens to the company, and I would like to find out if there's any connection between Englhardt and those two characters who broke into the office."

"I wouldn't be at all surprised." Her lip curled slightly. "They're all nothing but a bunch of Communist gorillas."

I leaned back on the couch and for some time contemplated her in silence. What had happened to these two very definite, very vital personalities, I asked myself, that weekend? When she first went out with Englhardt she had thought him charming. Now he was a gorilla. Which was the last epithet I would have chosen to throw at him. Swindler, maybe. But gorilla, no. To me, he didn't have that type of mentality. But then, I reminded myself, I'm not a woman.

"Think back, if you can," I said, shelving her personal feelings for the moment, "and try to remember exactly what he said about the company or about me."

She shrugged. "We hardly discussed business. Certainly, if he mentioned anything it was only to wish us continued success or some such generality."

"And he didn't appear to be worried about anything? You know, the reason he had come to Luxembourg was to discuss those dud motors they sold us."

She nodded. "Brent told me. But I can assure you he never mentioned them to me."

I stood up and paced the room. "All right," I said finally, "give it to me as gently as you can, but don't worry too much about my feelings. What happened between Friday night and Monday morning to change Englhardt from a charmer to a gorilla?"

"Why are you so anxious to know?" she asked softly.

I paused in front of her and stared down at her. "I assure you it's for no personal reason. I took a purge when I was in New York and got you, I hope, out of my system. I want to know because there are things happening to the company which I don't like and I have a suspicion Englhardt is involved. And it appears to me there must be some connection between the fact that you can't mention the man's name now without snarling and the fact that two of his compatriots broke into the office and had a good look at our records."

Her eyes suddenly shifted from mine, but not before. I had caught a glint of fear. And when she reached across to pick up a cigarette, her hand trembled. But she said nothing.

I sat down on the arm of the couch beside her and put my hand on her shoulder. "Did he laugh at you?" I asked, and when I felt her body stiffen, I knew I had struck somewhere near the truth. But why was she afraid? If Englhardt had refused her proferred charms and had been insensitive enough to boom out with his hearty laugh, I could understand why she would be furious. And she would certainly hate him. But why would fear enter into it?

Finally, I gave up. She wouldn't talk and no matter what leading question I tossed her, she turned it aside. But I eventually reached the conclusion that the Spa weekend had nothing to do with the two investigators from Moscow.

It was after midnight and I said I had to go. She stood up and moved close to me and her eyes asked me to stay.

"Get some sleep," I said, "and don't worry."

She put her hands on my shoulders and turned her face up to mine. "You once asked me to marry you. Is the offer still open?"

"Why? Are you feeling placid and faithful and ready to be bored?"

Talon-like, her fingers dug into my shoulders as she buried her face against my chest. "Please, oh please don't leave me! Or take me with you, now, tonight!"

Gently, I brought her hands down and held them in mine. "You look as though you haven't slept for a week, and I was riding a plane all night. So how be we postpone this discussion of our personal relationship until tomorrow?"

She drew her hands out of mine. "As you wish," she said, her voice almost a whisper. "Goodnight." But there was no love, nor even affection in the look she gave me as I opened the door. There was nothing but fear.

The next day I was sitting in my office when the midmorning mail arrived. Vera had remained home; she had phoned in earlier explaining that she didn't feel well and was staying in bed. And as yet there was no word from Brent. Miss Gaudin, who was completely oblivious of the undercurrents which were tearing at the foundations of the company, brought me the letters, and when I recognized the handwriting on one of them, I dropped the rest and tore it open.

Inside the envelope was a small piece of wrinkled brown paper—it might have been wrapping paper—and on it was scribbled a single line:

Take care of yourself—someone has informed.

I leaned back in my chair with a block of ice slowly forming in my stomach. I stared at the note. There was no signature; there didn't have to be. I would have recognized Englhardt's flamboyant scrawl anywhere. I picked up the envelope. It bore an East German stamp but even with a magnifying glass I couldn't make out the smudged postmark. The envelope had been folded and wasn't too clean. It looked as though it had been carried in someone's pocket before being smoothed out and mailed.

For a long time I sat there, staring with unseeing eyes at the warning he had sent me. Why, I asked myself bitterly, had I been so quick to lose faith in him? Why had I been such a blind fool and not realized when those two inspectors came to the office it was because they'd caught up to him and were searching for evidence? And why—and I cursed myself—had I rushed off to New York to lick my wounded pride instead of staying here to see him? Perhaps even then he knew they were closing in and I could have at least helped him escape. I clenched the note in my fist and slowly pounded the arm of the chair. He'd not even had the time or freedom to write to me from Brussels. Or he'd been afraid they would intercept the letter and come after me. East Germany—a military airport, no doubt, where the plane taking him back to Moscow had stopped to refuel. And he'd been able to slip the envelope to some friendly mechanic. Even on his way back to God alone knew what fate, he had taken the risk of warning me.

I smoothed out the note and like a hammer, the importance of those last three words suddenly struck me. *Someone has informed.* What did he mean? If one of his superiors in Brussels or Moscow had suspected he was receiving a cut from the Duchamp Company, surely he would have said they were suspicious, or that they had found out. He must mean someone outside the Ministry of Trade.

Carefully, I sifted through the names of every person I'd had dealings with in relation to Englhardt's affairs. Dmitri Smirnoff I dismissed immediately. One by one I ticked off the men to whom I'd sold the platinum. Many had guessed where the metal had come from, but not one, and I was ready to stake my life on it, had the slightest reason for even knowing Nicholas Englhardt's name. What about his friend, the *chargé d'affaires* in Bern? No. I reminded myself that he was as deeply involved with the platinum as Englhardt. And in Russia, he had carefully explained, one doesn't turn state's evidence.

That reduced the list of suspects to the staff of the Duchamp Company. Brent knew Englhardt simply as the Soviet official who handled our affairs at their embassy in Brussels. He had not, to my knowledge, even met him. Moreover, even if he suspected Englhardt was giving us preferential treatment, why should he complain ? He'd been making more money than any of us so far. And if his conscience was beginning to bother him because he was selling Russian goods, he wouldn't have been so upset over his inability to get rid of the electric motors.

Miss Gaudin, I didn't even consider.

Which left Vera. And I finally faced up to the fear that had been gnawing at my vitals since I first opened the letter.

Had she paid him back for whatever happened that fateful weekend by denouncing him?

But—and I tried to be fair—what did she know about Englhardt's private agreement with me? Unless I talked in my sleep, I'd never said anything about the platinum. In fact, I'd had a phobia about even mentioning that metal ever since I'd purchased Duchamp. My letters from him I'd meticulously destroyed as soon as I'd read them. Not only here, but in Paris. And any letters I'd sent to his private address, I'd written by hand and posted myself.

Or had he told her himself during that weekend how we were working together? I couldn't believe it. Englhardt didn't strike me as the type of man who would entrust his fate to a woman he was spending a weekend with. Even if she was my secretary. I recalled the act he'd put on that time he visited the office.

So if it was Vera, what evidence did she have? Or did she just suspect—and I didn't underestimate her intelligence —and write an anonymous letter to the Soviet Ambassador in Brussels and suggest that they look into the activities of the Duchamp Company, particularly in its association with Englhardt? Knowing the Russians, I had a strong suspicion that would be sufficient for them to recall him and set the MVD to work on us.

I shoved the note into my pocket and stood up.

There was only one way to find out. I started for the door and the telephone rang. Brent said that he had tried everything except breaking into the embassy, but he couldn't get a line on Englhardt. They wouldn't even admit that he'd ever worked there. They'd pulled down the Iron Curtain for sure, he said with a dry laugh. I told him to give up and come back to Luxembourg.

Vera opened the door on the chain. But the expression I was wearing must have frightened her. She asked me to please go away since she wasn't feeling well, and she'd telephone in the morning.

I stepped back. With a hefty kick I tore the chain's screws out and the door slammed open. I walked in, carefully closed the door and twisted the key.

"That makes it simpler," I said. "Now you know I know all about it."

She stood in the middle of the room, her hands covering her mouth, her eyes dark pinpoints of terror. "What do you mean?" she cried.

"What did you tell the Reds about Englhardt?" I rasped, trying to control my blazing anger.

She straightened up defiantly, and I had no doubt now of her guilt. I hit her with my fist. She fell against the couch and pulled herself up. The defiance in her eyes had changed to naked hatred.

"You bastard!" she muttered and I hit her again. This time she stayed down.

"What did you tell them?" I yelled, and felt myself trembling.

"What difference does it make to you?" She spat the words out. "Have you become such a party-liner—"

I reached down and grabbed a handful of flesh and negligee and jerked her to her feet. "Try to understand," I said, controlling my voice with supreme effort, "it's quite possible that I'm going to kill you. But if you don't tell me what you said about Englhardt, I'm going to beat that beautiful body to a pulp first."

She glared up at me, her expression full of contempt, and with no reaction whatever I watched the welt on her jaw redden.

"Who did you write to or talk to?"

Still she refused to speak and I slapped her face hard. "Tell, me, you slut!" I was shouting now. "Don't you know what they'll do to him?"

"I hope he gets what he deserves!" she snarled.

I tightened my grip on the negligee, but she must have seen the look of madness in my eyes. With a sudden, violent jerk she tore herself loose and ran into the bedroom, leaving the filmy cloth in my hand. By the time I reached the door, she was crouched beside the bed like a wounded tigress. In her hand was a small, blunt-nosed automatic. She was holding it very steadily.

"Now get out of here!" she said, and each word was a missile.

Suddenly completely drained of all emotion, I went back into the living room and threw myself into a chair. She followed as far as the doorway and stood there, her naked breasts heaving, the gun pointing at my face. And I realized now that because of some revengeful, sadistic twist in my make-up I'd always wanted to hurt her. Englhardt had simply been the excuse. I knew, actually, that any physical pain I might inflict would never make her confess.

For a long time we were silent while the tension, like the embers of a dying fire, gradually disappeared. "Perhaps I should have explained," I said quietly, "that Englhardt is more to me than just a Soviet trade official."

"I gathered that." Her voice was flat. "He was the reason you formed the company. What were you doing, splitting the profits with him?"

"I'd had dealings with him before." My mind was beginning to think rationally again, and I realized that I had to find out if she knew about the platinum. Because if she had told the Russians about that, then Englhardt was certainly beyond even God's help.

"I don't know anything about what you two were up to before, but it didn't take me long to figure out what was going on through the Duchamp Company."

"But I told you when I offered you the job that we were going to handle Russian goods. Did you decide then that you would denounce us when the first opportunity came along?"

Her lip curled. "What kind of a person do you think I am?"

"Quite frankly, I don't know. All I do know is that you've denounced Englhardt."

"If seeing that one of your Communist playmates gets his just deserts can be called denouncing, then I guess you're right."

She tossed the gun down on a chair, walked over to a cabinet and took out a bottle of whisky. "You've got quite a punch," she observed drily, pouring out a drink.

"Better make that two." She handed me a glass and sat down. "Why don't you go and put something on?" I said with sudden maliciousness. "I didn't come here exactly to make love."

She glared at me, her eyes full of scorn, and lit a cigarette.

"Before you went to Spa you knew Englhardt was a Communist. But you still liked him. You must have, or you wouldn't have been willing to spend a weekend with him. Now you're trying to sell me a bill of goods that you turned him in because he's a Red. How stupid do you think I am?"

She sat there, slowly sipping her drink, and I was reminded of an extremely beautiful Delilah in a bordello waiting for the next client. I found myself tired and disgusted with the whole messy business, including my own share in it. But to try to save Englhardt I had to know how much of the truth, if any, she had told them. Because from the moment I opened his note of warning and so realized I'd lost faith in him, I'd decided I would even go to Moscow if necessary to try and help him.

"All right," I said, "let's leave personal recriminations out of this and get down to facts. You went away with him not caring whether he was Khrushchev's young brother. But you didn't appreciate that all he wanted was a cheerful companion to discuss Russian music with while he filled in an otherwise dull weekend waiting for me. You took one look at his powerful body and turned on the sex. But for the first time in your life, you met a man who for reasons I can only imagine was not susceptible. That's fine. I can understand it, I can appreciate your violent reaction and there's been enough written about a woman spurned. You return to Luxembourg and decide that no man is going to make a fool out of you and get away with it. So you write to the Russian Embassy. I doubt if you had the nerve to go and see them. You tell them if they check into the activities of the Duchamp Company they'll discover that it has been receiving preferential treatment from one of their officials, and that undoubtedly the company must be making it worth while for this official. You're smart enough to know the Russian mentality. You were born with a good share of it. And you know that all you had to do was whisper 'graft' and Englhardt would save himself a lot of unhappiness by shooting himself."

"That was quite a speech," she said with more bravado than I think she felt. "And since you know all the answers why don't you get the hell out of here?"

"Don't rush me." I hunched forward in my chair and fixed my eyes on hers. "It so happens that I believe deep down inside you, you're sorry you did it. The other night you asked me to marry you. Why? I'll tell you. Not because you loved me, but because you were miserable. You hated yourself. You were desperate when you realized the terrible consequences of this vicious thing you'd impetuously done. You wanted someone to comfort you, to put his arms around you and tell you that everything was going to be all right. And you were afraid, not because a couple of Red goons were snooping around the office. No. You were afraid that I'd find out what you'd done, and so would Brent and Miss Gaudin and everyone else. You were afraid that we would not only find out what you'd done, but the real reason for your doing it."

Her glance dropped away from mine and for a long time there was only the remote sound of the traffic from the street below as she stared down at her knees. Finally I got up and sat down on the arm of the couch beside her and put my arm around her.

"Help me to help him," I begged softly. "What did you tell them?"

She raised her head and her eyes were glazed with tears. She got up and drew a book out of the bookcase, turned it upside down and shook it until a folded paper fell out. I picked it up and opened it. It was a carbon copy of a short, typewritten letter to the Ambassador, USSR Embassy, Brussels. Almost word for word, it was what I'd accused her of writing.

Carefully, I refolded it and put it in my pocket. "I suppose it could have been worse," I murmured. "At least you've given them no details." I stood up.

"Do you think you can help him?" Her bruised face was very close to mine.

Slowly I shook my head. "I don't know. I'll try from this side, and if I can't, I'll go to Moscow."

"But they will arrest you, too!" Her voice was full of concern.

I looked down at her. There were neither tears nor hatred in her eyes now. I knew that if I didn't get out of that apartment within the minute, I'd loathe myself for the rest of my life.

CHAPTER SEVEN

I T WAS DARK when I returned to the office but Brent was still waiting for me. I told him that I had finally heard from Englhardt that morning, but I didn't go into details. If I was to help the Russian, I knew I would have to play it alone and, as he had so ably taught me, close to the chest. I did tell Brent that circumstances had arisen which forced us to wind up the company. But since we had invested so much money in those motors, he was to keep on trying to get rid of them. I left it entirely up to him to set whatever price he thought he could get.

I caught the night train to Paris and was waiting in Dmitri Smirnoff's office when he arrived next morning. He took one look at me, told his secretary not to disturb us and closed the door.

"So they've found out." It was a statement more than a question.

"They know," I admitted, "but they didn't find out. They were told."

"Good God! Told? But who else knew about it?"

"My secretary. She didn't know but she guessed." And I explained about the fateful weekend and the disastrous consequences.

"Did she mention the platinum?"

"No. If she had I wouldn't have bothered coming here for your advice."

Dmitri leaned back in his chair and for several moments tapped his fingers together in silence. "It would appear," he said at length, "that because of his ignorance of women, our friend has got himself into a rather painful situation."

"And that," I said drily, "might be called the understatement of the year. But Miss Maudet is a rather unusual type—besides being half White Russian."

"Ah ha!" he snorted. "I am beginning to understand. A woman spurned is one thing, but a White Russian spurned by a Red Russian is, as the Bard might have said, a horse of a vastly different color."

"I hadn't thought of that," I admitted. "Anyway, that's the picture. What do you think I can do to help him?"

Dmitri pursed his full lips together and slowly shook his head. "If they've already got him back to Moscow, I don't know. How far are you willing to go?"

I thought his question over. How far was I willing to go? If Englhardt, surely realizing his perilous and vulnerable position, was foolish enough to antagonize a person whom he knew was not disinterested in his affairs, why should I stick my neck out and try to save him? On the other hand, it was my secretary who had denounced him and my fault for not taking greater care that the activities of the Luxembourg company were completely camouflaged. And I wasn't forgetting, nor was I particularly proud of my hasty decision in New York that he had been playing me for a sucker.

I glanced up at Dmitri. "I guess I'll go as far as I can," I said quietly.

"Personally, I cannot see how you are morally obligated," he said, his round eyes holding mine. "However, if that is your decision, I presume you have your reasons and I can only advise you to take very great care." He leaned back in his chair. "Well, let us see what you can do to help him. Did they discover any incriminating evidence in your records?"

"No. Nothing but the official correspondence relating to the dealings we've had with their Ministry of Trade."

"Good. Then I suggest your first move is to tackle the lion in his den. Call on the Ambassador in Brussels, show him the copy of the letter your secretary wrote and reveal enough of the story to explain why she wrote it. Tell him your books are open for his inspection at any time, and that you sincerely hope this irresponsible act on the part of a flighty female is not going to interfere with the successful commercial activities from which you are mutually benefiting. Don't evince any particular interest in Englhardt or his fate. Let the Ambassador assume that you are simply worried about losing their business."

"They're a pretty clammy outfit when they want to be," I said, and told him about Brent's failure to reach them.

"You can only try. The Russians will consider you very naive, but never mind that. They might wittingly or unwittingly give you some indication as to what has happened to our friend."

"And if they don't?"

"You'll have to go higher."

"You mean—Moscow?"

He nodded slowly.

The next day I presented my card to a thick-shouldered *fonctionnaire* in the outer office of the Soviet Embassy in Brussels and explained that I would like to see the Ambassador. He asked me to sit down and I cooled my heels for one hour. Eventually a slender young man dressed in a suit that looked as though he had slept in it came out and inquired as to the nature of my business. I carefully explained who I was, what our company had been doing for the Russians, and that some difficulties had arisen which I was sure the Ambassador would wish to hear about. He smiled politely and said that His Excellency was out, and would I care to come back the next day. I did—as I did every day for the rest of that week. But I never got farther than the young man in the rumpled suit.

I took it out on the Mercedes and made Paris in three hours, frontier included. But again frustrating disappointment was waiting for me. Dmitri Smirnoff had left for his vacation and, like most Parisians, wouldn't be back until the end of August. I could have gone to the Cote d'Azur and seen him, but for what purpose? Since I'd failed to leap even the first hurdle on this side, he could only advise me what I already knew: that it was time I got to work on the other side of the fence.

I picked up some clean clothes and remembered that there was still one man in the West who might help me, at least advise me—if he would. And that was Englhardt's accomplice in the platinum deal, the *chargé d'affaires* in Bern in whose account I'd deposited almost half a million dollars. But as I slammed eastward, impatiently cursing the crowded summer highways, I prayed that the time I was wasting in following up these leads wouldn't result in my reaching Moscow too late.

At the American Embassy in Bern, I checked the diplomatic list and discovered that the USSR *chargé d'affaires* was a Boris Kozloff and that he'd been appointed more than two years previously. But I recalled the fruitless days hanging around the Belgian Embassy and decided to approach Kozloff from a different angle. I asked one of the American secretaries what the next official diplomatic function was in Bern, and learned that the Swiss were giving a cocktail party and garden fete two days hence to celebrate the national holiday. I explained that there was a high Russian official I wished to meet for business reasons, but that I was afraid if I went through the usual channels I'd never get through to him. He understood, and finally said that since these functions were very large, very general affairs, I could tag along with him.

When we arrived there were five or six hundred people milling around the spacious rooms of one of the ministries, and with only that fleeting glimpse I'd had of the driver of the platinum car to go on, I began to fear I wouldn't recognize Kozloff if I met him face to face. And after an hour of quiet circulation, I was sure of it.

And then, when the guests were beginning to thin out, I caught sight of the woman who had been sitting in the front seat of the Sunbeam.

I asked her in French if she wasn't Madame Kozloff and she responded with an engaging smile and the fact that she was. I introduced myself and said that I was most interested in meeting her husband, and was he at the party. He was, she said, and led me over to a group of men in a nearby corner. She put her hand on the arm of a small, dapper, middle-aged man with a dusky complexion and black, Georgian eyes, drew him away from the crowd and introduced him. I had considered this individual before, but forgetting the fact that he had plenty of money to spend on himself, I'd dismissed him mainly because of his well-cut clothes and mundane manner.

We spoke of generalities for a few minutes until his wife drifted off, and I suggested we refill our glasses. From the bar, I guided him out to a quiet section of the garden and, without further preliminaries, admitted that the reason I wished to talk to him was in regard to a mutual friend, Nicholas Englhardt. But if I'd thought the mention of this name would alter even momentarily his bland, politely interested expression, I was mistaken. Not even so much as an eyelash flickered.

"Englhardt?" he said. "Don't think I know him. Who is he with?"

"He is—or was—one of your commercial attachés in Brussels," I explained, my eyes holding his.

He nodded. "Quite possible. Our commercial department has been expanding so rapidly these days I find it difficult keeping trace of the new men. You say you know him?"

I began to flounder. I had not expected him to admit to even the slightest knowledge of our platinum deal, but I was not prepared for this flat denial that he'd ever even heard of Englhardt. "May I ask," I went on, "were you in Bern last April?"

"April?" He thought for a moment. "Yes, yes of course. Why?"

"In that case I must tell you that I was the man Englhardt met that Sunday you and your wife took him out on a picnic."

His calm eyes never left mine, nor did his now slightly bored, slightly puzzled expression alter and I began to wonder if all Russian diplomats were recruited from the stage. "I'm afraid I don't quite understand what you mean," he said.

"Look, Monsieur Kozloff, I'm the last person to expect you to break down and admit to me, a complete stranger you meet at a cocktail party, something that I'm sure you don't even admit to your wife. However, Englhardt is in trouble and I'm indirectly responsible and I'm going to help him if I can."

Slowly, he shook his head. "I'm afraid you've mistaken me for someone else." Casually, he glanced over his shoulder and I could see that given the slightest opportunity, he would be off.

"I don't think so." I spoke hurriedly. "It so happens that I saw both you and your wife in the car with Englhardt that Sunday and—"

"Really, Monsieur—?"

"Sherman, Philip Sherman."

"You must excuse me, Monsieur Sherman. I see my colleagues are preparing to depart."

I was becoming frantic. "Give me one more minute," I begged. "To my knowledge, no one knows anything about the reason you went on that picnic, so relax. Englhardt is in trouble because his superiors suspected he was giving my company preferential treatment in the purchase of Russian goods and they naturally assume he was getting paid for this service. As I explained, I am indirectly responsible for their suspicions. They've recalled him to Moscow, and I had hoped that you might be able to advise me how I can help him."

"The only advice I can give you is to suggest you write to the Ambassador in—where did you say his last post was? Brussels? And explain everything."

My impatience changed to quick, blazing anger and I wanted to wipe that suave expression off his face with my fist. With some difficulty I controlled my voice. "Monsieur Kozloff, as I said before, I am going to do everything, repeat, everything I can to clear him or at least get him out of Russia. And I don't care who gets hurt in the process. I hope you understand me."

He set his glass down on a nearby bench, but even my implied threat fell as flat as the champagne in the bottom of his glass.

"This friend you mention," he said easily, "is very fortunate to have such a stalwart champion." He started towards the building.

I caught up to him and handed him my card. "I will be staying at the Bellevue Palace for the next couple of days," I said, "so if by any chance you can recommend me to someone in Moscow, some friend of Englhardt's, I'll be most grateful."

Casually, he accepted the card and dropped it into his pocket. "Perhaps we'll meet again," he said politely but without enthusiasm. "But I'm afraid I'm not the man you are looking for."

I stood there and said nothing. But I felt like climbing onto the nearest table and shouting out the platinum story to the assembled diplomatic corps of Bern. I had little doubt that that would shake this fancy-looking, Kremlin official's iron poise. I also had no doubt that it would tighten the noose around Englhardt's neck.

So I just left the party.

Two days later I was listlessly packing my suitcase and wondering what to do next when a page boy entered the room and handed me a letter. The address was typewritten on a plain white envelope and it had come via ordinary mail from Lausanne. I tore it open and inside was a small sheet of paper on which was typed a single name and address. The name was Petor Petrov and the address, 44 Pouchkine Street, Moscow.

And despite the fact there was no explanation, no advice, not even a line of comment—simply the name of one man in a country of two hundred million—my dejected spirits soared. Hastily, I retracted the sulphurous observations I'd been repeating to myself over the past forty-eight hours about Boris Kozloff's character and antecedents. I drove to Geneva, put the car in a garage and caught a plane to West Berlin.

"How," I asked an official in the U.S. Government office in Berlin, "does one go about getting into Russia?"

"Depends for what purpose. If you're selling, it's not easy. If you're buying—for dollars—they'll put you on the first plane and probably pay your fare. Or if you're an ordinary tourist, go across to the Russian Intourist office in East Berlin and they'll give you a visa without any difficulty."

I decided to apply for a visa as an ordinary tourist. I had little doubt that Philip Sherman, the director of Duchamp, Luxembourg, was on their black list, so if I applied through their commercial department for a visa, they'd either give me one and arrest me when I reached Moscow, or would simply refuse with no comment. But if I applied through their tourist office and gave my lawyer's address in Connecticut, I assumed that the departments were sufficiently separated that even if they did discover who I really was it would not be until I had left the country. Tourists were going to Russia by the thousands now and I hoped that, for a few days at least, I'd be considered just another starry-eyed visitor coming to see the results of the Great Experiment.

The Intourist agent gave me several papers to fill out, and when I had completed them, he attached my photograph to them and told me to return in a week. Surprised, I explained that my vacation was almost over.

He shrugged and said that last year it would have taken three months.

"You mean you have to send this information to Moscow?" I asked apprehensively.

"We'll get them out today by air," he promised. "But we've never had an answer back yet in less than a week. Of course, if you are willing to pay for it, we can ask them to cable their advice. Might save a day."

I had my hand on my wallet—and then withdrew it. Why call any more attention than necessary to the fact I was trying to get into Russia? If I hoped to be considered an ordinary tourist, I'd better start acting like one. I said I'd come back in a week.

CHAPTER EIGHT

SEVERAL FRENCHMEN, a young English couple, a most incongruous pair of elderly, world-trippers from Minneapolis and myself formed the group of Moscow-bound tourists which boarded a Sovoflot plane in East Berlin ten days later. My fellow countrymen were brother and sister and they reminded me of a pelican and a sparrow. He was tall, lean and cadaverous with calm blue eyes, while she was short, plump and fluttery. Five minutes after I'd met them she told me he was seventy-three and she sixty-nine, that they spent their lives wandering along the back roads of the world and that they'd been to Moscow the year before. As soon as I heard that, I attached myself to them, and during the long flight learned a great deal about what a foreign tourist can and can not do in Russia. One could move freely about Moscow and its environs, they explained and, provided the necessary permits were obtained, it was possible to travel through most of the country. They themselves were only staying a day or so in Moscow as on this trip they intended to explore the Crimea and later catch a ship to Istanbul. He asked me if I spoke Russian, and when I said I didn't know one word, he said that it was better—the officials preferred tourists who didn't under-stand the language.

And when I asked if foreigners were still subjected to close police supervision, he gave me a rather curious look and explained that everyone with whom I would come in contact, even the maid who brought up the morning tea, was associated with the police in one way or another. This bit of information sent a cold shiver down my spine, but I was nevertheless grateful to learn it.

At Moscow airport we were greeted by an extremely attractive, curvaceous blonde bursting out of an Intourist uniform. She spoke several languages, including perfect English, and appeared to be a person of authority. She shepherded us through the police and customs and I was interested to note the deferential manner in which these officials treated her. I had been told that all Intourist employees were secret police agents; the blonde must have been well up the ladder of authority.

The atmosphere at the airport was one of pleasant welcome and gradually I lost the sense of foreboding which had been building up ever since the plane had touched ground. I noticed no hard-eyed men in black suits watching me from around corners, nor bull-necked gorillas in uniform separating me from the curious proletariat. The police official who checked my passport gave me a broad, open-faced smile and said something about *Amerikanzi*. I hadn't the remotest idea of what he was saying, but from the tone of his voice I gathered it was pleasant.

The airport was a bustling hive of activity and in the waiting crowds was every type of Russian from beady-eyed Mongols in ill-fitting, nondescript sackcloth to young Muscovite jet-agers in Madison Avenue-type suits. The women, with the exception of our hostess, were disappointing. They were short and broad-beamed, with thick bodies and peasant faces. Make-up, when it was used, was often startlingly applied and the general costume consisted of a sweater or shirtwaist and skirt and flat heels. Foundation garments, if they existed, appeared to be in short supply with the result that hips rolled and bosoms bounced without restraint.

We were driven in a shiny new motor coach to the city and deposited outside the Sovietskaya where I had not only reserved a room in Berlin, but had to pay for it. I handed my passport to the desk clerk and was shown up to a large, comfortably furnished room overlooking a square. I sat down in a chair, put my feet on the window sill and, watching the onion spires of the churches melt into the twilight, asked myself what I was going to do now that I had arrived.

During the recent, busy days, I'd been too determined to get to Moscow to let the formidable task of even locating Englhardt discourage me. But now, as I gazed out across the darkening roof-tops of this mysterious, hostile city, the thought struck me with considerable impact that I was about as well equipped to rescue that big Russian as a mouse trying to rescue his brother from an angry bear. I didn't speak the language, nor could I even read the Cyrillic alphabet sufficiently to make out such necessary things as street names. I was a foreigner with, so far as the Ministry of Trade was concerned, a questionable reputation, and I was start-ing out on a mission that I knew my own government wouldn't lift a finger to support. My only asset was the name and address of an unknown character who might be a friend of Englhardt's. Of course, he might be an MVD official, tipped off with some phony story by Kozloff, and waiting to silence me forever with a one-way ticket to Siberia.

My spirits sagging, I got up, washed, and went down to the bar. I ordered a vodka, turned to survey the smoke-filled room—and almost dropped my drink.

Vera Maudet was sitting on a couch in a distant corner.

Automatically, I started towards her, and stopped. Sitting beside her was a well-built young man. From the way their heads were together, they weren't discussing the weather. Despite his well-cut clothes, he looked like a Russian. She was wearing the green Cairo number and it was obvious from her companion's expression that he was in the process of losing his scalp.

I turned back to the bar and tried to figure out what the hell she was doing in Moscow! True, her attitude towards Englhardt had softened sufficiently to give me the copy of the letter she'd written, but when I'd left her that last time in Luxembourg it was with the feeling she wasn't very sorry for what she'd done to him.

Which means, I told myself, that she hadn't come to Russia on his behalf. And knowing her attitude towards Communists, I was certain she wasn't just having herself a Russian holiday. And who was the young man?

I ordered another drink. But by the time I had finished it, I still hadn't thought up a good reason for her being within a thousand miles of this particular bar. I glanced over my shoulder. They were oblivious of everyone but themselves and I was confident that she hadn't recognized me in the crowd pressing around the bar. I slipped out into the lobby with the thought that I'd better consider this new twist to my destiny very carefully before I announced myself.

"What's to see. in this city?" I asked the concierge, and he handed me a thick guidebook in English. "That makes it simpler." I smiled. "Is it all right if I wander around alone?"

His eyebrows lifted. "Why not? If you get lost—" he unfolded the map in the guidebook "—there are taxis here, and here, and here." Each time he said "here" he circled an intersection on the map with his pencil. "They will bring you back to the hotel."

I walked out into a soft, humid evening without an idea of what direction I was following, my mind a jungle of disconnected thoughts. The only thing I was sure of was that Vera Maudet and Nicholas Englhardt were in Moscow, and that there must be some sinister connection, some relationship between them that she hadn't wished to reveal and he hadn't been able to. I was full of apprehension.

The sidewalks, even the roadways were crowded with citizens out for the evening air. The few motorcars, like snowploughs, literally pushed their way along, and now that they were not permitted to use their horns, the progress was snail-like. No one paid me any particular attention; in fact I'd felt more conspicuous in many a Western city. I had no idea whether I was being tailed, but it couldn't have been easy to do in that crowd.

The first bright bar I came to I went in and chose a quiet table. The waiter didn't understand me. Finally he shrugged and went off. I decided to sit there anyway for a few minutes and got out the guidebook and opened the map and shoved Vera into the back of my mind. The waiter reappeared with a big smile and a bottle of beer in one hand and a bottle of vodka in the other. I chose the vodka and he poured out a glassful.

Pouchkine Street, I discovered from the map, was a long thoroughfare halfway across the city from the hotel. It was already nine o'clock and I didn't want to do anything as obvious as riding there in a taxi, so I decided that Petrov would have to wait until morning. There was a restaurant connected to the bar and I realized I was starving. Through the connecting doors I noticed a large table spread with *zakuski,* and since this would eliminate any language difficulties, I went in and chose a tasty cold supper.

The tempo of the city had long since dropped into low gear but as I twisted and turned on the wide bed, sleep persisted in evading me. Finally I said to hell with it, put on my dressing gown and leaned out of the window. The night was heavy and hot and the dirty gray sky seemed to be resting on the bulbous church spires. Like misplaced eyes, there was a light here and there in the black mass that was the Kremlin, but the great red stars had been switched off and with the exception of the dull street lamps, the rest of the city was in blackness. It seemed to me incredible that down there were three million souls, sleeping, snoring, making love; at this hour there were more lights on in Ashtabula, Ohio.

I was suddenly aware of a soft but persistent scratching on the door. Carefully, I opened it an inch. Vera was standing in the hall. She came in, closed the door and slipped the bolt across. I drew the curtains.

"What, may I ask, are you doing in Moscow?" I thought I had whispered, but she put her finger to her lips and nodded towards the bathroom. She went in, turned on the cold water tap in the bathtub and sat down on the only convenient fixture the bathroom provided. I closed the door behind us and leaned up against it.

"Most of these bedrooms are wired," she said in a matter-of-fact tone of voice. "Give me a cigarette."

I handed her one and lit it. She was still wearing the green dress, but her hair had been done up less carefully. There was a soft, feline expression in her eyes and the jealousy I thought I'd at last conquered knotted my stomach. "Okay," I said, "what are you doing in Russia?"

"Why shouldn't I come here?" She stared at the cigarette. "I resigned from the company after you left and—well, now that some barriers here are down, I decided to come and see what they've done to the land of my forefathers."

I moved closer to her. "As you have said, the room is probably bugged. So why waste words telling me a lot of nonsense? You're here for a definite purpose. What is it?"

She glanced up at me and there was an impish smile playing around the corners of her soft mouth and no matter where she'd been that night I wanted to take her in my arms.

I jammed my fists into the pockets of the dressing gown. "Did you change your mind and come to Moscow to make sure Englhardt got what you think he deserves?"

Slowly, her eyes holding mine, she shook her head. "No. I came here because I was afraid you would get into trouble. You don't know these people. Nobody in the West does. In your naive innocence, you probably think that all you have to do is hire a smart lawyer and bail Englhardt out."

She went on talking, but the rest of her words were meaningless. She had come to Moscow to help me! My blood began to pound.

"You love me that much?" I asked tenderly.

"Love?" She stood up and ran her hands down her thighs, smoothing out her dress. "What's love got to do with it? I put you into this mess and the least I can do is try to make sure you don't get into a deeper one."

"Mighty considerate," I muttered bitterly, and I would have given my right arm to have been able to retract my question. "But I assure you I'm perfectly capable of looking after myself."

She put her hands on my shoulders. "Why do you go on fighting yourself—and me? I don't like your friend, but since you insist upon playing Sir Galahad, I am willing to help you. At least I speak the language and I have a sneaking suspicion it's going to require more than just your enthusiasm to prevent them from giving him the full treatment."

As I stared down at her I knew that she was absolutely right. It was going to require something more than wishful thinking to help Englhardt. This man Petrov, for example. Suppose he understood nothing but his own language? I could hardly take along an interpreter and ask questions about Englhardt.

But was she here really to help me? In view of her mother's former nationality, it was a tremendous risk even during these enlightened days. A risk no intelligent person —and she was certainly that—would take without a powerful reason—unless she loved me. And yet when I mentioned love she had all but laughed at me …

"Stop beating your brains out," she said, "and let's go to bed. If they're listening in, and we don't, they'll be suspicious as to why I came to your room."

"At least you've discovered a new excuse."

"You are a bastard at times, aren't you?"

"Besides, I'd an idea you'd already been to bed once tonight."

Her eyes, half closed, were smoldering. "Does it make any difference to you?"

"Not any more." I shrugged. "How do we all compare?"

If someone was listening in, the crack as she slapped my face must have split his eardrums. I stepped back and ruefully rubbed my jaw. "You've got quite a wallop yourself," I complained, suddenly grinning at her. "I think perhaps I will accept your offer. You could beat off the wolves while we race for the frontier."

"Corn, at this hour of the morning, is indigestible."

"I'm serious."

And I was. Not only was I serious, but for the first time I had discovered that behind her calloused façade she was vulnerable and a wave of tenderness drove the bitterness out of my mind.

"Well, this is neither the place nor the moment to discuss your plans," she said, turning off the tap.

The hammering rain awakened me and I got up and closed the windows.

"What time is it?" she asked.

I switched on the lamp and glanced at my watch. "Six-thirty and it looks like a good day for ducks."

"I'd better go."

"You staying in this hotel?"

"Of course. It's where they put most of the foreigners. Makes it easier for them to keep an eye on us."

"In that case..."

She didn't go back to her room.

By ten o'clock the rain had ceased and a hot sun broke through and soon dried the cobble stones. Pouchkine Street proved to be a narrow thoroughfare with solid blocks of dingy-looking apartment houses lining either side. I walked slowly past 44. It looked the same as all the others and, without going up and asking the concierge, it would be impossible to find out which apartment, or even which floor Petrov was on. There were no letter-boxes in the entrance. Presumably, if they existed, they were inside the concierge's cubicle. Recalling that I'd been told all these concierges were petty police agents paid to keep an eye on the activities of their tenants, I was afraid that if a foreigner inquired for Petrov, not only would I be under suspicion, but more importantly, Petrov would undoubtedly receive a visit from the MVD.

If there was a telephone in the building, I doubted whether there would be more than one public one. Besides, I couldn't even read the directory!

Frustration mounting, I walked back to the hotel. It seemed to me so completely incredible that here I was in Moscow and afraid to walk up and knock on a man's door and say hello.

Vera was in the bar having a drink with the English couple from the plane. I joined them. I listened with little attention to their excited description of what they'd seen that morning, and as soon as the opportunity arose, I suggested to Vera that it was time we were going.

At the hotel entrance the doorman gave me a smug glance as he opened the door for us, and I presumed, like every other member of the hotel staff, he knew who had been where the night before. I was beginning to acquire that feeling of living under a magnifying glass.

"Going where?" Vera asked, when we were in the street.

"For a walk. I assume the trees are not yet wired for sound."

I explained about Petor Petrov. But I didn't explain how or where I had learned his name; simply that he was a friend who might know something about Englhardt.

"Do you want me to go and see if I can find him?" she asked.

"No, you're too well dressed—too obviously a foreigner."

"What about sending him a note suggesting a rendezvous?"

"How can I be sure it's him when he turns up?"

"That's a point."

For some time we strolled along in silence. And for the first time since I'd arrived in Moscow, I noticed the passers-by pausing to stare at us. But it wasn't me who caught their attention. Vera, with her long blond hair coiled around her head and her golden complexion looked as Russian as they. But here the comparison ceased. With her svelte figure and smart suit, her sheer nylons and high-heeled, open-toed slippers, she was like a breath of the Rue de la Paix. But there was no envy in the glances that lanced her way; admiration, yes, and even fascination. But more than anything else the sight of her walking down the street seemed to give these drearily-dressed citizens a tiny lift as, when passing an open doorway, one suddenly hears a few bars of beautiful music.

My thoughts must have communicated themselves to her for finally she said, "Let's face it—there's only one way to contact this man. I'll go and take off this Marie Rivetti suit and call on him."

"I don't like you taking the risk."

"Where's the risk? I was told last night I haven't the slightest accent."

I hung around the hotel for the rest of the afternoon waiting for her to return. And as the hours passed, it was with difficulty I restrained myself from getting a taxi and going to see what had happened to her. At six o'clock she walked into the bar, and I don't think even her companion of the night before would have recognized her. She was wearing a rough tweed skirt, a tight-fitting sweater and over bare feet were battered sandals. Her hair was still coiled around her head and her face was shining with that scrubbed-with-soap-and-water appearance. The only difference I noticed between my ex-secretary and the hundreds of other young women on the street was about ten inches around the waist.

We sat down at a corner table and I told her I'd been worried sick.

"I had to hang around until he returned from work," she explained.

"Talk to him?"

"Not possible. My God! Three people—he, his son and daughter-in-law all live in one tiny room. You can't imagine! And they seemed like very decent, well-educated people. Ugh!"

"And so?"

"Tonight at eight-thirty I'll show you where to wait in Lenin Park. If he thinks it's safe, he will join you."

"Does he speak English?"

"Perfectly. And French."

I put my hand over hers. "What would I have done without you?"

"Don't thank me yet," she said quietly. "This game might prove a lot more dangerous than we think."

"What makes you say that?"

"Petrov's manner."

At eight-thirty I was sitting on a bench in a secluded corner of Lenin Park. Vera had left; she explained that Petrov had insisted I be alone. The bench I was sitting on was one of those double-sided affairs and a few minutes after Vera disappeared, an elderly, heavily built man emerged from the shadows and sat down with his back to me.

"What is it you wish?" His voice was soft, cultured and reminded me of Englhardt's.

"Nicholas Englhardt," I replied in an undertone, resisting a strong impulse to twist around and look at him.

"You are too late."

The quiet, definite, matter-of-fact statement turned my blood to ice water. "You mean—?"

"He's been sentenced to fifteen years' hard labor."

"But he's still alive?" The relief in my voice must have been obvious.

"If you call it life," he said with quiet reproach. "Why didn't you stop him from coming back?"

"I couldn't. I didn't know until it was too late. Did he speak of me?"

"He is very fond of you. In fact, he was more worried about what might happen to you than he was about his own predicament."

"Where is he now?"

"In the Crimea working in the mines."

At least, I said to myself, it's not Siberia. But what difference it would have made, I didn't know. "It happened so quickly—only three weeks!"

"What is there to take up time? After he was brought back, he was charged, tried and sentenced all in one morning."

"He put up no defense?"

"What defense does a guilty man have?"

"He told you everything?"

I felt the man shifting on the bench behind me. "I must leave you now," he said.

"Please, a minute more. Can I get a message to him?"

"I will send it. Whether he will receive it or not, I don't know. But in any case you must remember it will be censored."

"I understand. When can I see you again?"

"I don't know. Why did you come to Moscow? There is nothing you can do." His voice was full of resignation.

"I had to find out whether I could help him."

There was a long pause. "Do you know the Gorky Park?"

"I will find it."

"Tomorrow night, then. In the southeast corner. I will try to be there at about this hour."

I felt him standing up, but when I glanced over my shoulder his back was towards me and I couldn't see his face. He shuffled off into the shadows and my only impression was that he was very old or very tired.

The next morning I hung around my room, impatiently waiting for the hours to pass. But when I went down at noon and the manager asked me if I was feeling well, I thought I'd better begin to conform to the usual tourists' routine and took a guided tour of the city in the afternoon. But the beauties of modern Moscow were completely lost on me. My mind was too busy considering the information I had learned from Petrov the night before.

Fifteen years in a prison camp—fifteen years chipping ore in a mine! Each time I thought of it, anger and frustration welled up within me like bitter bile and I wanted to lash out and destroy those who had done this to him. I carefully avoided Vera, and although she had left a note asking me to call her, I was afraid of what I might do if I saw her again.

I detested myself for ever touching her, for even speaking to her after I had discovered that she had denounced Englhardt. What would he think—I tortured myself with the question—if he knew that the first woman I'd held in my arms after reaching Moscow was the woman who had betrayed him?

I returned from the tour and tried to compose the message I would send to him. It was not easy. What could I say? That I was sorry that for the next fifteen years he'd be in a prison camp? Or that I was leading an armored brigade down to rescue him? I regretted that they had not stopped me at the frontier, that they had let me into their cursed country.

Long before eight-thirty, my impatient feet took me to Gorky Park. I made sure which corner was the southeast, but didn't linger. There was no use hanging around there any longer than necessary. I was too obviously a foreigner among the crowds of men, women and children which filled the park. I wished that Petrov had chosen a more private place for the rendezvous. I wanted to see him, talk to him quietly face to face. I needed something more to take back with me from Englhardt's friend than just an impersonal voice.

As before, a few minutes after I sat down, he arrived and slowly eased himself down on the other side of the bench. The crowds were beginning to thin out. There was a smell of rain in the air and with sudden panic, I wondered what we would do if it came.

"It is kind of you to see me again," I said. "But is there no other place we can meet where it's more private?"

"I have been thinking the same thing," he said. "I would like to know more of the man in whom Kolia has so much confidence."

"You cannot come to my hotel? My room?"

"That would be too dangerous. But if you wish you can come to my home tomorrow. It is the sixth day and there is no work. Three o'clock is the best hour."

"Your concierge will not say anything?"

"In the afternoon he will not be there. But it would be better if the clothes you wear would be more in keeping with ours. You do not speak Russian like your friend?"

"No."

"Then don't speak with anyone."

"Do you know the address of the prison camp where he is?"

"Why?" I felt the bench move, but it was more of a snort than a chuckle he gave. "You are going to rescue him?"

"Well, no," I said lamely, not quite knowing myself why the information would help me. Certainly I could never write directly to him. They'd probably add another year to his sentence for each letter he received from a foreigner. As for rescuing him—admittedly I had come to Moscow with that idea in the back of my mind. But that was before I'd learned he was already sentenced and in prison.

"Empty your mind of such gallant thoughts, my friend," Petrov said. "I know that you Americans haven't the capacity to resign yourselves to the fate destiny has chosen for you. I suppose that is why you are, as a people, so refreshing—if unpredictable. But in this case you will save yourself much unhappiness if you will accept his fate, as he has, and return to your own land."

Before I could answer, a young couple strolling along paused, and glanced at the bench. There was nothing I could do but move over and make room for them. Smiling their thanks, they sat down beside me. A few moments later the bench moved and I knew Petrov had stood up. Casually, I glanced over my shoulder but he had already started towards the gate. I gave him a long minute, got up and walked slowly back through the gathering darkness to the hotel.

"Why are you avoiding me?" Vera demanded as I entered the bar. She was sitting at a small table just inside the door and obviously had been waiting for me. She was pale and her eyes were framed with tiny wrinkles of worry.

I dropped into the chair across from her. "I don't know," I muttered, my voice flat and depressed.

"I've been worried."

"Worried? About me?" I taunted. "You'd better start worrying about that big, handsome Russian you spent the weekend with in Spa. Did you know that little interlude has cost him fifteen years' hard labor?"

"Oh, no!" she cried and several people turned and stared at her.

"Take it easy," I said. "Perhaps we'd better have a drink." I called over the waiter.

"You're telling me the truth?"

I nodded, watching her. She had been pale before; now she was as white as a sheet and I could almost feel the sharp fingernails digging into her palms as she clenched her fists.

The waiter set a carafe of vodka and two glasses on the table. I poured the drinks and handed her one. She gulped it down, coughed and reached for a cigarette.

"But what can we do?" she asked some moments later.

"Frankly, I don't know," I replied bitterly. "The old man's advice is to forget about it and go home."

"But ..." Her voice trailed off and when I noticed the tears gathering in her eyes, the bitter hatred that had been warping my thoughts since the night before died away. I began to regard her as a child who had done something wrong and had been punished. It was senseless to go on punishing her forever. Besides, if there was anything to be done, I would need her help. In fact, I reminded myself, I need her help right now.

"I'm seeing the old man again tomorrow," I said, "at his home. You'll have to tell me exactly where the room is. He didn't have time tonight."

"Do you want me to go with you?" she asked quietly.

"No, there's no point. You'd better play the part of the wide-eyed tourist for the benefit of those who might be interested in us."

"And you don't think it's possible to do anything? Appeal, reduce the sentence or—"

"Now who's being naive? Once they put you in the mines I presume they forget about you. Especially our friend," I added caustically. "With his build they're not going to let him go in a hurry."

She bowed her head and covered her face with her hands.

"Come on," I said, motioning to the waiter for the check. "Let's go and find a bright spot to have dinner. I feel as low as you look but there's no use sitting around here thinking about it."

Petrov's tenement was a walk-up and he lived on the fourth floor. In spite of the fact I was wearing an open shirt and flannels which, after being soaked in the bathtub had been dried without benefit of an iron, I felt extremely self-conscious as I threaded my way through the half-dozen citizens lounging on the front steps. Their curious eyes followed me and one or two muttered what I presumed was a word of greeting.

Petrov must have been waiting just inside the door. The moment I knocked it opened. I slipped inside and he carefully closed the door before extending his hand.

"You're sure this won't get you into trouble?" I inquired anxiously.

"No, no." He reassured me with a gentle smile. "I am only sorry that one cannot be more gracious with one's hospitality."

I glanced around the tiny room and tried not to let the shock of horrified surprise show in my expression. Fortunately Vera had prepared me. But as I surveyed this room, this man's home, I found it incredible that intelligent people would accept living under such degrading, miserable conditions. And at last it was vividly, realistically brought home to me why Englhardt had been willing to risk everything, even his life, to lift himself out of such squalor by any means, fair or foul.

The single, curtainless window was wide open but it seemed to have no affect on the heavy, musty smell of human bodies. The principal furniture consisted of two lumpy beds, one wider than the other, against opposite walls. Under the window, in the narrow space between the beds, was a washstand and on it a jug of water rested in a battered tin basin. In one corner was a small iron stove which presumably served for cooking as well as heating. In the other corner was a chest of drawers, its top covered with faded framed photographs, books and a motley collection of chipped plates and glasses. Clothing hung from nails on either side of the door, and from the ceiling suspended a single, naked bulb. The walls had at one time been papered, but it must have been before the Revolution. The color had faded to a drab gray and here and there cracks were covered with rambling ribbons of brown paper. More time-yellowed photographs of public buildings—or they might have been large private houses—spotted the walls. Above one bed, like a rose in a refuse dump, hung an exquisite gold and red ikon.

There was one battered wooden chair and Petrov invited me to sit on it. He eased his bulk onto one of the beds while the springs protested. I took a package of American cigarettes out of my pocket and offered him one. With a polite nod he accepted it and, after admiring it a moment, carefully fitted it into a small, nicotine-stained holder. I brought out my lighter—and wished I'd had matches. It was a gold Dunhill and I was suddenly acutely conscious of how ostentatious it was.

Petrov leaned back on an elbow. "You are as I thought you would be," he said, pensively, after staring at me for several moments. "It is interesting how much a voice can reveal a man's personality."

And I in turn found myself studying him. He was a heavily built man, almost fleshy, the result no doubt of the common starchy diet. He was old, much older than I had imagined, and must have been eighty. But his close-cropped, iron gray hair was still thick and there was a youthful gleam in his clear blue eyes. His features were big and once again I was reminded of Englhardt. And his clothes, although mended many times, were clean and his shirt freshly laundered. I visualized his daughter-in-law carefully preparing him for this rendezvous with a foreigner.

There were many things I wished to find out about him and about Englhardt and his previous life. But I was afraid that despite his reassurance, my presence in his room would do him no good if it became known to the police. Without further preliminaries therefore, I spoke of the subject which had brought me to his door.

"The other night," I said, "you mentioned that Englhardt had explained everything to you. Did he say how we had started to work together?"

"You are referring to the platinum, of course."

"Yes. Did the authorities know about it when they sentenced him?"

"Fortunately for his sake, no." He puffed on the cigarette. "He would have been shot if they had."

"What was brought out at the trial?"

"I was not able to attend. But I learned that he was charged with using his official position to further his own ends."

"But they had no proof," I protested. "And unless he confessed—"

"He did not confess, but neither did he deny the charges."

"But why didn't he fight? At least make the prosecutor produce his evidence? They'd have soon found out there wasn't any."

Petrov carefully extracted the half-smoked butt of the cigarette from the holder and placed it on the washstand. "You must know Nicholas' character. He has always gambled with his life. When he wins, he is very happy and enjoys it more than most. And when he loses he never complains. He shoulders his misfortune and asks no man to share it with him."

"I understand. But when someone stacks the cards or deals a phony hand, even the most fatalistic gambler has the right to protest."

For some time we were silent and my companion's attention seemed to have drifted off. Now that I was here, I asked myself just why I was. If it were only to satisfy my curiosity about this friend of Englhardt's, it was a dangerous pastime. Or had I expected that eventually this elderly man with the calm expression and the cultured voice would rub some magic lamp and produce Englhardt for me? I didn't know.

"How, may I ask, did you get my name?" he asked finally.

"The third man in the platinum deal—Boris Kozloff."

"I thought it must have been Boris." He nodded his head slowly. "Now, there is a man who would fight back."

"I gathered the same impression. Not only fight but use any holds he could think of." I handed him another cigarette. "You must forgive my curiosity, but I have been wondering what your relationship is with Englhardt."

Petrov again went through the slow ritual of carefully fitting the cigarette into the holder before replying. "I was the director of the family's estates before the Revolution."

"It's strange, but when I heard you speak that first time, and even now seeing you face to face, I had the impression you were a blood relation. There is the same timbre, the same resonant quality in your voices."

A gentle smile lifted the corners of his wide mouth but he said nothing.

"You speak of estates," I went on. "I presume then, that Englhardt's family was not of the proletariat. He told me he was not a Communist, so how is it that he had a government position?"

"To answer your question intelligently," Petrov said, "I will have to tell you a little of his life, his background."

As the name implies, Petrov explained, Englhardt was a descendant of one of the powerful Swedish families which had come to Russia centuries ago and adopted Russian nationality. His family had always had great wealth with estates scattered from the Crimea to St. Petersburg and town houses in Moscow, Paris and Lausanne. He was brought up in the extravagant surroundings of those twilight days and spent as much time abroad with his family as he did in Russia. His father was killed early in the First World War, but it had little affect on the boy as he hardly knew him. Apparently Englhardt senior, like many aristocratic Russians of that period, would return home once a year like a giant, black-bearded Santa Claus, distribute lavish presents from the far corners of the earth, and be off again almost before the presents were opened. The strong influence in the boy's life was his mother. She had been a well-known beauty, as much at home in Paris as St. Petersburg and, from the tender, affectionate tone of Petrov's voice as he described her, I gathered that his had been one of the many hearts that had lain at her feet.

When the revolution broke out, Mrs. Englhardt and her son had escaped to Finland and thence to Switzerland where they decided to live. The Bolsheviks seized everything in Russia, but there had been sufficient assets outside the country to provide her with a comfortable life and the boy with an education. However, like many of the aristocratic refugees, she had no conception of the value of money and when she died in 1930, they were penniless. Englhardt scraped together what he could, and for the next nine years disappeared in South America.

Shortly after the Second World War started, Petrov went on, Englhardt suddenly turned up in Moscow and tried to warn anyone who would listen to him that Russia was in danger, that Hitler would one day turn his mechanized hordes eastward. The authorities eventually threw him into jail, ostensibly because he was a White Russian. Actually, Petrov claimed, they put him away because too many people were beginning to believe him.

A few months later Hitler marched into Russia. In the frantic search for cannon fodder, the jails were emptied and the prisoners forced into uniform. Englhardt found himself in a tank regiment and quickly rose from the ranks to command of a brigade at the battle of Stalingrad.

The war over, he discovered he was a hero, and since he'd proved his love for his country by voluntarily returning and fighting for her, they gave him a government job and put his foreign experience and ability to speak numerous foreign languages to work.

For the next five years he lived in Moscow. Which, Petrov said, was a mistake. If they'd sent him abroad sooner, he might have been able to endure the personal restrictions, the humiliating anonymity, the complete debasement of all human dignity which the Communist state required. As it was, when he eventually came and told him he was being sent abroad, Petrov knew that he'd never return willingly.

"But why did he have to stick it out here?" I asked. "Surely, after the war there must have been many opportunities to escape to the West."

"Mainly because of his love for his country. You see, during the war he was too busy soldiering to pay much attention to what Communism had done to Russia. Or if he did suspect that this was not quite the Utopia the propagandists claimed, he reminded himself that we were fighting a bitter war of survival.

Then came victory and the years of enlightenment. He discovered that the restrictions of war had become the oppressions of peace. So at last he decided to go. But now he was older and once across the frontier he would be penniless. And since he had nothing to offer the West—he was no scientist nor a police agent with secrets to sell—he knew that he'd be stuck in a refugee camp for a year or so until some charitable country accepted him. I can appreciate Nicholas' lack of enthusiasm for either a refugee camp or charity. It is not in his character. And besides"—again that understanding, quiet smile—"You must remember that he was brought up to know and enjoy the good things of life. And since the Communists had stripped his family bare, I presume he considered it poetic justice that they finance him now."

I glanced at my watch and noted with alarm that an hour had slipped by. "I am glad you have told me his story," I said, making ready to go. "It is much easier for me to understand many things. There is only one more thing I wish you'd tell me. I don't know what good it will do me—or him. But just exactly where is he now?"

"Near a port called Kerch in the Crimea. But J don't think it is a very good idea for you to write directly to him."

"I understand." I stood up. "The next time you write to him, say that we have met and that so long as I live I will be thinking of him."

Petrov heaved himself to his feet. "Perhaps one day all this will change," he said, taking my hand. And then, with a shrewd glint in the eyes which were so much like Englhardt's, he added, "But I shouldn't wait in Russia until it does. They might decide that you too should spend some time in the mines."

I walked slowly back to the hotel, reviewing in my mind the life of Nicholas Englhardt. Petrov had brushed in the missing strokes and at last I was able to view the complete picture. Now I understood why, in spite of the pride and love he had for his country, he had been willing to sacrifice forever his right to return to it. The reasons behind his desire to accumulate great wealth I had suspected; he was too much a man of the world, too sophisticated, not to have known a different life than that which existed in Russia today. And as Petrov had said, what the Communists had taken away, he felt no qualms about taking back. Just how guilty he was, I didn't know. I did know that I didn't feel the slightest twinge of guilt for helping him.

That evening while Vera went to the opera with the English couple, I borrowed a map and several travel folders from the concierge, took them up to my room and studied them. I'd vaguely heard of Kerch. I knew it was a port somewhere in the Crimea, but it was not until I checked the map that I discovered it to be the seaport at the entrance to the sea of Azov. What industry there would necessitate convict labor, I couldn't imagine. I had heard that the Crimea had been turned into a workers' holiday camp. A photograph in one of the travel brochures finally gave me a clue. It showed a cluster of sprawling blast furnaces in Kerch which indicated that somewhere nearby might be iron mines. I wasn't aware that in Russia convicts were working the mines. I'd had visions of frozen lumber camps in Siberia. However, it would appear that a workman is a workman whether he slept with his wife in a shack or alone in a prison camp.

As I studied the map further, I recalled the tour my elderly Minneapolis travelling companions were making. If they could explore the Crimea, why not me? I could even follow their footsteps and get a ship out to Istanbul. I had a thirty-day visa and I'd only been in the country four days so I had plenty of time.

Just what I was trying to accomplish by getting as close to Englhardt as possible, I didn't know. Certainly, I would never be permitted to see him. Petrov had warned me about even writing. But it seemed as though his personality, like a powerful magnet, was drawing me to him. I spent a restless night trying to understand why.

The next morning I had breakfast with Vera and told her I was leaving Moscow and that since I was anxious to see how Transeastern's affairs were going in the Middle East, I was travelling out via Odessa to Istanbul.

"You think there's nothing to be done, then?" she asked.

I shook my head. "Nothing. What's more, it's been suggested that I might find the climate more healthy elsewhere."

Her brow furrowed with anxiety. "You mean, someone has warned you?"

"Indirectly. And since once you were an employee of the Duchamp Company, I suggest that you also leave while the atmosphere is still cordial."

"What can they do to me?" She shrugged. "But why do you take the long way around? That means you'll be in the country that much longer."

"Look at a map. The shortest distance between here and Turkey is not via Berlin."

For several moments she stared at me, a tiny frown of perplexity clouding her expression. Finally, she opened her bag, took out a package of cigarettes and carefully lit one. "Do you mind if I go with you?" she asked casually, blowing out the match.

"I don't think it's a good idea. If they pull me in you might get caught in the net."

"When are you leaving?"

"As soon as possible." I stood up. "Where will you go? Paris?"

"I suppose so," she said quietly. "Will I see you there?"

"I'll call you up when I arrive."

"Yes, do."

We might have been complete strangers who had spent a fleeting moment together.

CHAPTER NINE

I T REQUIRED all of the morning, but when I left the Intourist office, I had a travel permit which entitled me to go to Sevastopol, a ticket and a reservation on the plane leaving that night at eleven o'clock. After lunch I forced myself to take another conducted tour of Moscow and wondered if there'd ever been such a disinterested visitor to the city before. Later, with an inexplicable sense of foreboding—I was carrying Petrov's warning around like a nail in my shoe—I checked out of the hotel and took the bus to the airport. The police inspected my papers with complete disinterest; nevertheless, I waited impatiently for the plane to take off.

And if it had been possible at that last moment to alter my flight from Sevastopol to Berlin, I would have. I found myself suffocating for a breath of freedom.

It was ten minutes before eleven when Vera arrived in a taxi. And when I noticed her luggage I knew she had not come to say goodbye.

"I decided," she explained with exaggerated casualness, "to have a look at the Crimea myself."

"I might have known." I shrugged. "Well, since you no longer work for me, I can't tell you what you can or cannot do." But deep down inside me, I was glad to see her. There was something very reassuring about her presence. I felt like a nervous swimmer starting out to cross unknown and dangerous waters and suddenly finding a life belt under his hand.

The trip south was lengthy, boring and uncomfortable. Despite the much-ballyhooed progress in Russian aviation, our plane was a travel-weary DC-3, or fair copy, and the broiling sun was already high when we finally reached Sevastopol. The Intourist agent at the airport took us in hand and escorted us to the hotel where we were given two large rooms overlooking the Black Sea. The beaches were crowded with humanity, and I had the feeling that if we hadn't been foreign tourists spending dollars, we wouldn't have found a bed on this vacation-jammed peninsula. We went for a swim before lunch but the water was soupy.

"Is he down here somewhere?" Vera suddenly asked, after we'd stretched out on the hot sand.

"You mean Englhardt?" I knew perfectly well to whom she was referring, but since neither of us had mentioned his name after we left Moscow, I assumed that she had not guessed the real reason for my coming here. Her question jolted me.

"Of course," she said quietly. "That's why you're here." And then she added, "And that's why I came."

"You deflate my ego," I said wryly. "I thought it was because you ached to be with me."

She rolled over on her side and faced me and only with difficulty did the skin-tight, green bathing suit hold everything in. "And if it was?" she asked softly.

I stared at her for a moment. "Let's get back to your original question. Yes, he's here. Or rather a hundred and fifty miles away in an iron mine."

"Are you going to try and see him?"

"Good God, no! That would be fatal for him and maybe for me as well."

"Then I don't understand why you came and why you go on torturing yourself."

I shook my head. "I don't understand either."

"You don't think there's a chance of getting him out?"

"You mean," I asked in amazement, "help him escape? Lord no! I've never seen a Russian prison camp, but from what I hear, they're not institutions you can walk out of easily even with outside help. Besides, supposing he did escape, he's still got to get out of the country and the frontier must be four or five hundred miles away."

Her eyes lifted and she stared out across the Black Sea. "You're wrong," she said slowly. "The frontier is just out there—where the sea meets the sky."

"It's a long way to swim, even in this warm water," I put in drily.

"And down there in the harbor are ships," she went on as though I hadn't spoken. "It's quite possible that some of them are foreign."

"Huh!" I snorted. "You've been reading too many suspense stories."

Suddenly she stood up. "What about some lunch? I'm famished."

There were two ways to go to Kerch overland, the hotel manager told me after lunch. One was to hire a car, which worked out to about a dollar a mile. The other way was to go by bus. Either way, I had to return inland to Simferopol as there was no coastal highway. He was not at all surprised at my proposed journey, and suggested I make a side trip from Simferopol to Yalta. The bus, he explained, departed at six o'clock in the morning, and with any luck I should reach Kerch that night.

That afternoon, Vera and I wandered down to the port. A new city was slowly emerging from the ruins left by the Germans; Hitler's hordes had had to level Sevastopol stone by stone before the embattled defenders, after months of resistance, were wiped out. This city, I recalled, had added a stirring page to Russian history, and it was unfortunate that the memory of such valiant deeds had been tarnished by the subsequent actions of our former allies.

None of the ships we saw wore foreign flags. They were mostly coastal steamers; small freighters and passenger ships catering to the workers' paradise the Crimea had become. Even we, foreigners with passports and exit permits, would have to go to Odessa to find a ship for Istanbul. The hope that had flared in my mind that morning when Vera had mentioned ships promptly turned to ashes.

I told her I was going to Kerch the next morning and asked her if she wished to come. She wondered if it were wise to go, and I replied that it was perfectly natural for us to tour the peninsula.

It was not long after leaving Sevastopol that I regretted not hiring a car no matter what the expense. The bus we were riding was a battered, vintage diesel with a leaky exhaust, and despite the fact that the windows were either open or missing, both of us soon had headaches. It was jammed to the roof with good-natured locals who, after discovering that we were foreigners, insisted upon giving us the front seat so that we could see their country. They were distressed that we hadn't brought along any food and in spite of the early hour, plied us with smoked fish, garlic sausage, black bread and a very heavy, sweet white wine. When Vera explained that it was just their idea of a breakfast snack, I looked forward to lunch with some apprehension.

We soon left the pine-clothed slopes behind and ran out across a wide, treeless plain. The crops had been harvested and the golden stubble fields lay sleeping in the hot, glaring sun. At Simferopol, after shaking hands with practically every passenger, we changed busses and headed into the east. For the remainder of that long, weary day, we bounced the breadth of the peninsula, stopping at each dusty village and often in between. Most of the time the road ran like a wandering ribbon across the sun-drenched, dusty plains, now and then curving southward into the cool forests clothing the foothills of the mountains to seek out some hidden hamlet.

And to add to my discomfort was my disappointment. I had heard that the Crimea was the Cote d'Azur of the Black Sea. Perhaps along the coast, beyond the mountains, it was. But from my hard seat all I saw was mile after mile of very dull steppe, dried up river beds and impoverished villages. Even the people, tough, wiry-looking citizens, their skin darkened by sun or Tartar blood, thinned out. The thought passed through my mind that if Englhardt ever did manage to escape, he should be able to hide out forever in this sparsely populated land.

We arrived in Kerch in time for a late supper, but the reservation I'd asked the hotel manager in Sevastopol to make either had not been received or else it was the only space available; we had to share a hot, stifling room the size of a matchbox with a young couple from Zaporozhye. They were very pleasant, very natural, and very much in love and I finally got to sleep with my head under the pillow.

The next morning we discovered a café overlooking the strait and had breakfast.

"Well," Vera said, "now that you're here, what are your plans?"

"Find a room with a little more privacy," I replied. "This communal living is not for me."

"You'll get used to it." She laughed. "He probably thinks you drink too much."

"Is that what he said when you were talking to him this morning?"

"No," she replied with an impish grin. "Something much worse."

"Don't be vulgar. Look, let's not waste any more time than we have to in this overcrowded holiday camp. These iron mines where he's supposed to be are to the northwest of the port. I'm going to hire a taxi and drive out that way."

She leaned towards me. "Let me get this straight. Are you just satisfying some pernicious quirk in your nature by having a look at his prison camp? Or is there, floating around somewhere in the back of your mind, the idea that maybe you can help him escape?"

For a long time I stared at her. "To be quite honest, I find it difficult to answer your question," I admitted finally. "Ever since yesterday, when you mentioned the frontier is the sea, the idea of getting him away has been growing, certainly. But—"

She stood up. "In that case the first thing for us to do is go see for ourselves how impregnable these camps are. But I suggest instead of taking a taxi—if there is such a thing in this part of the world—we rent a couple of bicycles. They'll look more natural."

We pedalled out beyond the sprawling blast furnaces and Vera had been right about not bringing a car. There wasn't one in sight, but there were dozens of bicyclists and no one paid us the slightest attention. And once again my mind reverted to the matter of escape. Englhardt would either have to walk, or ride a bicycle!

Not far beyond the port the slag heaps began, but before we could get close to them, we were stopped. A high wooden gate stretched across the road and on either side, curving away across the sun-baked, barren ground, was a barbed wire fence twice a man's height.

There was a wooden shack beside the gate, and in front of it, in the shade of an eave, a guard was lounging. The shirt of his dun-colored uniform was open, exposing a hair-matted chest; carelessly resting on a forearm was a snubnosed tommy gun. When we stopped, he eased himself off the wall and sauntered towards us. He was young, open-faced, with straw blond hair and a thick, powerful body.

Vera spoke with him for some time in Russian and I gathered from their gestures that he was telling her how to get around the camp to the country beyond. Casually I turned my bicycle around and, out of the corner of my eye, surveyed the prison camp. A hundred yards beyond the wire fence were fifteen or twenty long, unpainted wooden shacks and I judged these to be the prisoners' quarters. On the other side of the shacks were the mine buildings and hoists. At intervals along the fence were spindle-legged watch towers, but as far as I could tell, they were empty. In the midst of the huts rose a central tower, higher than the others, and I caught the glint of sun on searchlights. I couldn't see the opposite side of the enclosure but it must have been half a mile away. Near the mine buildings a score of men were working, but they were too far distant to recognize their features.

Vera and the guard were laughing together now, and he was holding up her bicycle. It was obvious from the light tone of her voice that she had turned on the charm. I drew further away and inspected the surrounding country. Like the enclosure, it was bare earth and rocks; the authorities could not have selected a more desolate, sun-scorched site. I recalled having thought that Englhardt was fortunate in being sent to the Crimea, but I believe I would have preferred the snows and tundra of Siberia. The whole area was in a slight depression and even the sea was not visible.

But as for escaping—it seemed to me that on a stormy night and armed with a pair of wire-cutters, it should not be difficult. In fact, it looked so simple, I searched around for the catch. I soon discovered it. Two heavy cables, obviously the power supply for the mine, paralleled the road we had come along. And from the nearest pole to the gate two lines branched off and down into the guards' hut. The wire was much too heavy, I thought, to be used simply to supply light to the shack. I was right. From the rear of the building, cables led out through a series of heavy insulators and were connected with the fence. And it was apparent from the size of the insulators that the current which ran through that fence must be of considerable voltage.

With a final burst of laughter, Vera turned her bicycle and started back up the road. I grinned at the guard, and he said something to me. I nodded, got on the bicycle and followed her.

"I thought you were trying to buy the place," I said, when we were well out of hearing. "What went on?"

She was still smiling. "It's too bad he's not the commandant. We'd have your friend out of there tomorrow."

"Another scalp?"

"He comes from Moscow and he's lonesome and he thinks the women down here are all Turkish cows."

"How did you explain my presence?"

"I said that you were a stupid pig from East Germany who didn't know a word of Russian and that I was your official interpreter."

"Thanks! And you think he believed you?"

"Why not? Fortunately you didn't open your mouth, and I doubt if he's ever seen an American before."

"What else did you find out?"

"About the camp? Nothing. I didn't ask. But he wants me to meet him tonight at the Young Soviet Club. Apparently it's the only gay spot in town."

For several minutes we pedalled along in silence. "I don't know whether I like it," I said quietly.

"Like what? If you're going to help Englhardt, we'll have to use every trick in the bag."

"Sure, but I don't want you to get involved."

She laughed. "You mean, don't you, that you don't want me to become involved with that blond Russian giant."

Anger flaring, I glared at her, hit a pothole and almost went over the handle bars. "Dammit!" I muttered. "Why don't you go back to Paris and let me take care of this alone?"

"And just how far do you think you'd get?" she taunted.

I just didn't answer.

That afternoon we found a cubbyhole with a lumpy bed in a flea-bitten hotel near the port. But we were the sole occupants and at that moment it looked like a room at the Ritz. We went for a swim in the lukewarm waters of the strait, had dinner, and while

Vera was keeping her date at the Young Soviet Club, I wandered around the docks. I discovered no foreign ships, but I did come across a small excursion boat unloading, and when I mentioned Sevastopol to one of the sailors, he said. *"Da,"* and I made up my mind that when we returned to Sevastopol, it would be by sea.

In one corner of the harbor were grouped a fleet of fishing vessels and suddenly I found my heart beating faster. If I could help Englhardt escape—the idea now had become a definite decision to attempt it—why not hire, or better still, steal a fishing boat? Once across the sea we could have it returned and the owner compensated. It was summer, the sea was calm and the coast of Turkey little more than two hundred miles away. I didn't know much about boats, but there was little I didn't know about engines, including marine, and provided we kept heading south, we were bound to strike the Turkish coast.

While the idea jelled, I moved closer and inspected the vessels. They were mostly deep sea trawlers, much too big and too complicated to steal. But amongst them were several smaller boats—and this was only one section of the harbor.

The more I considered it, the more sure I was we'd have to pirate a vessel. The skippers of these ships had the freedom of the seas at their disposal, and they must be trusted men. Or else a commissar accompanied them to make sure the ship always returned to port.

I wandered back to the hotel, completely forgetting in my excitement that I hadn't even begun to think of how to get him out of the place to begin with.

It was three o'clock when Vera returned. I had long since tired of sitting in various cafés and had turned in. Silently, she slipped out of her clothes, switched off the light and crawled into bed. She appeared to be dead tired and more than a little drunk.

"How did you get on?" I asked.

Turning her back to me, she moved over to the very edge of the bed. "I only hope you think that bastard is worth it," she mumbled, and a moment later I knew she had fallen asleep. I lay there for a long time wishing that platinum had never been discovered.

She was still asleep when I got up next morning. I dressed quietly, went down and asked the hotel manager, who understood some German, how often the ships ran to Sevastopol. He explained that in the summer an excursion boat went up one day and returned the next. The next one would be going to Sevastopol that morning. He thought they sailed around nine.

As it was not yet eight, I got a bottle of mineral water and returned to the bedroom and awakened Vera. I handed her a glass of the water and a pain-killer. She swallowed the pill and gulped down the water.

"God!" she muttered. "What a night!"

"Sorry to get you up so early," I apologized, "but there's a ship leaving for Sevastopol and I want you to be on it."

She tossed the long golden hair back over her bare shoulders. "What?" Go back to Sevastopol? Why?"

I sat down on the edge of the bed. "There are about five hundred reasons. But I guess the most important one is that I don't intend to sit around here like a conscious cuckold while you take on the guards of the prison camp."

She glared at me, her eyes blazing. "You should complain! All you have to do is nurse that precious jealousy of yours. I have to cope with those sex-hungry brutes!"

"Exactly," I said quietly. "That's why I want you to leave."

"Give me another glass of water." I handed her one. She drained it and leaned back against the pillows. "Whatever you wish," she said, her voice suddenly listless. "If you don't think he's worth it, it's all right by me. And the sooner we get out of this godforsaken country, the better I'll like it."

"I'm staying."

"Still playing Sir Galahad—" her eyes were scornful "—with your little wooden sword."

"Okay, okay." I stood up. "You haven't too much time."

"Oh, for heaven's sake! Forget about it." She kicked the sheet off, swung around and put her bare feet on the floor. "Did you discover where the plumbing is in this firetrap?"

"Two floors down."

"I might have known it."

I waited downstairs for her, but it was long after nine when she appeared. But I'd already given up any idea of forcing her to leave. She would go only when I did; of that I was sure. And I was also sure that having once seen that prison camp, I'd never leave until I'd at least made one good try to get Englhardt out.

It was a clear, sparkling day and we walked down to the same café on the waterfront and ordered breakfast. And as though by mutual agreement, neither of us mentioned Sevastopol again.

"He's there, all right," she said after the first cup of coffee. "At least, the description fits. Those goons last night didn't mention names, but they were talking about a convict they called 'the giant' who'd arrived two or three weeks ago and who had money to spend."

"That sounds like Englhardt. Especially the money part." I smiled grimly. "Trust him to feather his nest even in a prison camp. What else did you learn?"

"Well, they work twelve hours on and twelve hours off, some of the galleries are knee-deep in water, every so often there's a cave-in, and to date no prisoner has left the mine alive."

"Good God! That explains why they have to use convict labor to work it!"

"I suppose so. Even the guards refer to it as the death hole."

"What did they mean when they said he had money to spend?"

"Apparently the guards aren't too strict. There are no political prisoners there which means there are no ideological barriers. No one has ever escaped; either it's too difficult or it's no use—they'd only be picked up trying to cross the isthmus to the mainland. Besides, after spending twelve hours below it seems that one has little interest in anything but getting drunk if possible, or going to sleep. Englhardt arranged—don't ask me how, but apparently it's not unusual —to get some money into the camp and he's made a deal with one of the guards to supply him with vodka."

Slowly, my thoughts racing, I nodded my head. When I knew Englhardt, he was not what I would have considered a drinking man. A bottle of champagne once in a while; wine, yes. But to go to the trouble of smuggling in money, and the risk of bribing a guard to keep him supplied with vodka, didn't make sense. Perhaps in another year or so when despair replaced hope—but not so soon. No. It sounded as though he had something on his mind. And there could only be one thing—escape. If I could only talk to him, find out what he was planning...

I leaned across the table and covered her hand with mine. "I don't know how you did it," I said with warm admiration. "But you make Mata Hari look like a third rate chorus girl."

"Thanks," she said drily. "But I'd prefer working in the chorus."

"Is there any way we can get a message to him?"

She shook her head. "I was afraid to ask or to show too much interest. There were four or five of them together, but one nasty type didn't drink. He had his mind on something else."

"You, I presume."

She looked away without answering.

"What do you suggest as the next move?" I asked.

"Get hold of the guard he's bribed."

"How many are there? Guards, I mean."

"I don't know. But there are over five hundred prisoners."

"Say ten to a guard—makes fifty. Not easy to find him."

"But if he's interested in extra money, presumably it's because he likes to spend it. Which means he should turn up at the club sooner or later. It's the only bright spot in town."

"How much longer can you stand it?"

She gave me the full benefit of her tawny eyes. "How much longer can you?"

When she went back to the club that night, I walked out the road to the prison camp. It was a blaze of lights. Fixed beams were directed on the wire fence; from where I stopped, it looked as though a mouse couldn't crawl through undetected. There was no activity around the mine buildings, which I presumed meant no night shift. A group of men were gathered around the main gate, and when two or three of them broke away and started walking toward the port, I beat a hasty retreat.

That night Vera returned early. But she wasn't tired, she'd been drinking very little and was in a gay mood.

"I've made myself expensive," she laughed, getting undressed. "I asked them to buy me champagne and when they said they couldn't afford it, I called them a bunch of Ukrainian *moujiks* and left. You should have seen their faces!"

"I don't blame you," I said approvingly. "To hell with those goons. We'll figure out another approach."

"No," she protested. "You don't understand the Russian mentality. They'll go back to camp and talk about it. And they'll raise the money somehow and be back tomorrow night. Or they'll bring along a man who has money."

"I'm beginning to get it. In other words—"

"I won't be surprised if the man Englhardt is bribing comes along to see just how expensive this sophisticated woman from Moscow really is."

"I wish there was more I could do than just sit around while you take all the risks."

"There is," she whispered, snuggling into my arms.

The next day I concentrated on working out an escape route. For some reason I was confident that Vera would locate the guard and that we would be able to get a message to Englhardt somehow. And the least I could do was to have everything pre-pared on the outside. I turned in the battered bicycles we had rented and bought new ones. They cost almost the equivalent in dollars of a small Fiat, but I wanted no irate owner complain-ing to the police if we and his bicycles suddenly disappeared. In the afternoon I cycled out toward the prison camp again and inspected the power lines. The poles were wood and about twenty feet high. I figured that with tennis shoes on I was still young enough to shimmy up to the top. I stopped half a mile from the gate, turned off the road and from a slight rise made a rough sketch of the camp buildings and fence and marked in the watch towers. I rode slowly back towards the town until I discovered a narrow road which branched off to the south. I followed it and struck the main highway inland to Feodosiya, a town fifty miles away. The distance from the camp to the turnoff I estimated to be three-quarters of a mile.

I returned to Kerch and bought the largest pack I could find and in two separate stores, purchased two pairs of heavy cutting pliers with insulated handles. In the last store I also bought a kilo of short roofing nails with big heads.

Returning to the hotel, I left the bicycle in the entrance, and walked into the arms of two, heavily built men who had "police" written all over them.

"You are Mr. Sherman?" one of them asked in passable English.

"Yes," I said, acutely conscious of the pack containing the pliers and nails in my hand.

"You have your passport?"

I dropped the pack on a chair, reached into my pocket and got out my passport. The speaker took it, flipped open the pages and checked the particulars. "You are staying long in Kerch?" His voice was neither cold nor warm; it was completely imper-sonal with studied disinterest.

I shrugged and tried to slow up my pounding heart. "I don't know. It's very pleasant here and I thought I might cycle around the country a bit. Why?"

It was his turn to shrug. "There are many more beautiful places in Crimea than Kerch."

I tried on a grin. "Couldn't know that until I got here. Well, there's nothing like starting at the bottom and working up!"

They were not amused. "What relation is Miss Maudet to you?" It was the other one this time, and his English was even better.

"My fiancée."

"But you didn't come to Russia together," he said and I panicked. They must have interrogated Vera first. What had she told them?

"I followed her. At the last minute I couldn't get away, and since her passage was already booked—" I still had on the grin but it was wearing very thin.

"Where did you meet her?"

"Oh, I've known her for a long time."

"She speaks Russian very well."

"She should. Her mother was Russian. That's why she wished to visit this country. She'd heard that you people were beginning to accomplish great things in Russia and she wanted to see for herself."

Both men nodded and I felt I'd scored a favorable point.

"Is that why she spends so much time at the Young Soviet Club?"

"She's not going to learn anything about the country hanging around with me. She can do that at home." They remained silent, so I went on. "What's the matter anyway? Have we done something wrong? I thought you people were welcoming tourists now."

The man holding my passport gave me a Siberian smile. "We were just interested," he said, handing me back the passport. "You're the first American who has stayed here since the war."

"Well, I doubt if I'll be the last," I said with forced enthusiasm. "You've got a wonderful country here. What about a drink?"

"Thank you, no," he said. "Perhaps another time."

They shook hands very formally and left. And as I watched them waddling down the street in their baggy trousers and tight-fitting jackets I had the feeling that I was going to see those gentlemen again unless I got out of Kerch as soon as possible.

Vera was waiting in the bedroom. "Did you run into those goons?"

I put my finger to my lips. "You mean, those fellows downstairs? They're police checking up because we're foreigners. Seemed rather nice guys."

She nodded her head in understanding. "What about a walk before dinner?"

"Good idea." I put both pairs of pliers in my pockets and wished to hell I hadn't been so clever about buying the nails so soon. I couldn't very well wander around the town with them in my hands. And then I told myself that if they'd wanted to search the room, there wasn't much doubt that they had already done so.

"You think they've planted a microphone in the room?" she asked when we were in the street.

"Could be. Anyway, we'd better take no chances."

"What do you think is behind their visit? They'd seen our passports when the hotel keeper handed them in."

"They're trying to find out why you're so interested in that club, for one thing. And although we're obviously more than friends, I suppose they can't figure out why I don't mind you going there alone and beating it up with the boys."

"Which means they're keeping an eye on us. Had I better give it up?"

I walked along for some time in silence. "God! I don't know," I said bitterly. "We seemed to be getting so close…"

"But what can they do to us except throw us out of the country?"

"That's what's so devilish about these police states. You just don't know—until you're on your way to Siberia. What did they ask you?"

"The usual. When did I come to Russia, why, and where did I learn to speak the language and so on."

"I told them you were my fiancée."

"When are you going to tell me?" I sensed a note of wistfulness in her voice, but when I turned and looked at her, the smile touching her lips was impish.

"Whenever you're ready to hear it," I said quietly.

"We'd better be serious."

"I am."

"I mean, about the police. I'll go to the club once more tonight. After all, I promised I'd turn up and we don't want those guards coming around to the hotel looking for me. But if I don't get anywhere, we'd better give it up."

"And if anything happens—to you, I mean?"

She slipped her arm through mine and squeezed it. "In that case, you'll be free to look for a fiancée whom you can really love."

CHAPTER TEN

ONCE MORE I SPENT the night wandering from café to café waiting for her to return. At midnight I asked myself if Englhardt was worth it; if any man was worth what she was going through—putting herself into the hands of those drunken sots night after night. I didn't blame the police for beginning to wonder what kind of a man I was.

And at one o'clock I was cursing the country, Englhardt and myself. And I made up my mind that no matter what she discovered tonight, tomorrow she'd leave Russia if I had to carry her aboard the plane myself.

I was still waiting downstairs when she returned. "You feel like walking," I asked, "or are you completely worn out?"

"Let's walk for a bit. It's probably safer."

It was a hot, breathless night and despite the late hour, people were still wandering about the streets, no doubt postponing, for as long as possible the return to their overcrowded, stuffy bedrooms.

"I found the man," she said quietly when we'd moved away from the hotel entrance.

"Wonderful!" I put my arm around her shoulders and hugged her. "Was it difficult?"

"No. All he's interested in is money."

"Simpler. What did you say?"

"Oh, I gave him a long story about knowing the giant in Moscow, that he was an old boyfriend, and that since I was down here on vacation I'd like to send him a parcel of food."

"And he agreed?"

"He said it would be expensive, that there were others involved."

"The old story, but never mind. When do you see him again?"

"I don't," she said. "He gave me the name and address of a shop and said that I was to leave the parcel there with the necessary postage, as he called it, and it would be delivered."

"How much is this postage?"

"Four hundred roubles."

"Whew! He'll soon be able to retire. But how will we know that Englhardt actually receives it?"

"I asked the same question. He said that a receipt from him would be left at the shop a day or so later."

"Sounds like it's a regular channel. And you don't think he suspects anything?"

"No," she said. "Why should he?" And then she said, "Let's go back to the hotel. My feet are killing me. I had to dance with those heavy-footed louts for hours."

When the hotel was in sight, I asked, "And he wasn't surprised at your request? I'm sorry to third-degree you like this, but I'm taking over from here and I would like to know all the answers."

"You can have it," she said bitterly. "I wish I'd never met that big Russian bastard. In fact, I wish I'd never left Cairo."

I followed her up to the room in silence.

"To answer your question," she said quietly after she was in bed, "the answer is no. It was my impression that this pipeline into the camp existed long before Englhardt arrived. They all discussed it quite openly and casually which I'm sure they wouldn't have done if it had been set up only a week or so ago."

I spent part of the next morning wandering through the government-monopoly food stores looking at food. With the ration coupons Intourist had issued us in Moscow, I finally bought a tin of caviar, smoked salmon, several cans of what I gathered from the pictures were various types of seafood and a bottle of vodka. But it was not until I entered the last shop that I discovered what I was really looking for. It was an earthenware jar of the white cheese that is very popular in that region. It is not unlike cottage cheese, but much thicker in texture and I knew from experience much stronger in taste. However, what interested me more than the contents was that the jar had a screw top and was tall enough to hold the pliers.

Leaving the package of food at the hotel I went down to the Intourist bureau. The girl behind the desk inquired if we were comfortable and since it wasn't her fault there wasn't a decent hotel in the town, I said we were and asked about planes to Western Europe. It took her a long time to figure out connections and I guessed it wasn't a request she received every day. Finally she explained that I could take a plane from Sevastopol to Kiev via Odessa, change planes at Kiev and go out to Vienna via Lvov. If I was willing to pay for the telegrams, she could have reservations by tomorrow morning. I told her to go ahead and book the passage in the name of Miss Vera Maudet for the day after tomorrow. Before leaving the bureau I changed two hundred and fifty dollars in travellers' checks for which she gave me a thousand roubles.

And then, on the spur of an inspiration, I called at the police bureau on my way back to the hotel. The several uniformed characters in the outer office stared at me with blank amazement when I inquired for someone who spoke English. The idea finally got through to them, and after I'd held down a hard wooden bench for half an hour, one of the plainclothesmen who had called at the hotel the day before appeared and asked me what I wanted.

I explained that Miss Maudet was leaving Russia in a day or so and I wasn't sure whether it was necessary to report it to the police. He asked me if she had her exit permit, and I said that she'd gotten it before leaving Moscow. In that case, he said, everything was in order and she could leave when she wished.

I was about to say thanks and goodday, when he said, "You are not going with her?"

"No," I replied. "She has to return to Paris and I am going to Istanbul on business. I thought I'd wander over to Odessa when she left and see if I can pick up a ship."

He nodded, his pale, flat eyes holding mine, but said nothing.

"Well," I said, grinning at him, "just thought I'd better let you know we're on our way." I shoved out my hand and after a moment's hesitation, he shook it. I felt his eyes boring into my back as I walked out the door.

On my way back to the hotel I offered up a silent prayer that if they suspected anything now that they knew we were leaving, they'd act right away and not wait until Vera was about to step aboard an out-going plane.

That afternoon I wrote a short note to Englhardt in English. I told him to prepare to escape and that beginning from the seventh night from now—I added the date—he was to watch for the camp's lights to go out at two o'clock in the morning. The moment they did, he was to cut his way through the south fence between the first and second watch towers counting from the gate. I explained that the current would be off the fence and that I would be waiting for him on the other side. If possible, he was to answer with a simple *da* or *niet*—about the only two words of Russian I was sure of—and under no circumstances was he to write anything in English. I didn't sign the note; I knew he'd recognize the handwriting.

And as I sat there, staring at the sheet of paper and wondering what else I should tell him, I tried to recall all the Hollywood prison-break productions I'd ever seen. Visions of Humphrey Bogart shooting his way over the wall while a sultry blonde waited at the wheel of a high-powered getaway car passed through my mind—and I began to appreciate how unprepared and ill-equipped I was to tackle the formidable task I'd set myself. The only thing I had was the blonde, and I sincerely hoped she wouldn't be around when the break was attempted. I had nothing to shoot with, a couple of bicycles instead of a car, and I wasn't even certain my Humphrey Bogart was Nicholas Englhardt!

Shoving aside these depressing thoughts, I wrapped the note around the pliers, emptied a small plastic bag I used for carrying a washcloth and put the pliers inside. I unscrewed the top of the jar of cheese, scooped out the center and pressed the pliers down into the clotted, white mass. I filled up the hole and replaced the top. The jar felt slightly heavier, but even when shaken violently, there was no sound of a solid object inside.

I had Vera write a note in Russian explaining that the food was a gift from a friend who had not forgotten him, and that she hoped he would enjoy his favorite delicacy, the cheese. I had a suspicion the note would be read by whoever smuggled the parcel into the camp, and I was afraid that if I called attention to any particular item, they might become curious and investigate it. At the same time, knowing Englhardt's generous nature, I could visualize him distributing the food among his friends one dark night. And if this type of cheese wasn't one of his favorite dishes …

"What do I do now?" I asked Vera when the parcel had been wrapped up with her note inside.

"Give it to me, and four hundred roubles."

"No," I said, "I'll take it. Where is this shop?"

"Are you crazy? You open your mouth and they'll know immediately you're a foreigner and they'll probably call in the police."

"But you won't be here to pick up Englhardt's acknowledgement. They'll have to give it to me."

"What do you mean, I won't be here?"

I sat down on the edge of the bed. "Just this. I've booked you a seat on a plane leaving the day after tomorrow for Vienna.

You're going to be on it. And that's final, definite and there'll be no argument."

"You think you can handle it alone?" The tone of her voice surprised me. It was very quiet, almost resigned. I had been prepared for the usual blast.

"I'm going to try," I said.

She shrugged. "In that case, you'd better come with me to the shop and I'll explain to whomever's there that they must give you the receipt. But don't say one word."

The shop proved to be a small food store. From the small amount and poor condition of the produce displayed for sale, I presumed it was privately owned. The prices, I knew, were much higher in these back-alley stores, but then one didn't need a ration book. Why the police permitted their existence, I didn't know. Perhaps they had to patronize these minor blackmarket outlets themselves to augment the rations they were allowed to buy at the government food stores.

A slatternly, middle-aged woman with dyed, henna-colored hair and enormous sagging breasts appeared from a curtained doorway at the rear of the shop, threw me a professional glance that had nothing to do with the sale of food, and asked Vera what she wanted. Vera handed her the parcel and said that Nikita would call for it. The woman nodded and held out her hand and Vera gave her the thick wad of roubles. Rapidly, she counted it, nonchalantly lifted a grease-spotted skirt and displayed a remarkably shapely thigh as she tucked the money into the top of her stocking.

Vera asked her when we might expect the receipt and she said to return the next night, that it might have arrived by then. But if not, it would certainly be there the day after.

"What a horrible creature!" Vera muttered when we were out in the street again.

I laughed. "I suspect they sell more than food in that shop."

"But to have to trust people like that! Why, she might even sell us out to the police."

"I doubt it," I said reassuringly. "After all, she's got a good racket, and I can't see the police paying much for information about smuggled food parcels."

"But if she finds out the truth?"

"Let's hope she doesn't." Or if she does, I added to myself, I sincerely hope it's after your plane has reached Vienna.

The next day moved as though it were two hundred and forty hours long. Intourist informed me at noon that Vera had a through reservation to Vienna and that her plane left Sevastopol the next evening at eight o'clock. She wouldn't arrive in Vienna until four the next afternoon which obviously meant considerable waiting around airports enroute. But the Intourist girl explained that it was the best connection she could get. Ordinarily I wouldn't have worried about it. But I knew all too well Vera's predilection for doing the unexpected and I didn't want her suddenly to get bored in Odessa or Kiev or somewhere else along the line and decide to come back and see how I was doing. Once she was in Vienna, I didn't care where she went. She could go on to Paris or go back to Cairo—the only place she couldn't go was back to Russia. She'd have to get another visa and by the time she had that, I hoped that I would be close enough to her to make it unnecessary. I decided to accompany her to the airport—at least I could make sure she actually got on the plane. However, I didn't wish to leave Kerch before that evening in case there was a message from Englhardt. Which meant a cross-country dash the next day in a rheumatic taxi, the only one I could find whose owner would agree to make the journey.

As that hot, sweltering afternoon slowly progressed, my spirits dropped in direct ratio to my mounting fear that this dangerous game I was playing was about to blow up in my face. I cursed my stupidity in rushing out to buy the bicycles. I would need them, certainly, but now that Vera was leaving I'd look pretty stupid keeping both of them. And I regretted my impatience in warning Englhardt to be ready in seven days. Getting him out of the camp was all very well. But beyond a hazy idea about fishing boats, I still hadn't a clue as to how I was going to get him out of the country. And after tomorrow night I'd be completely on my own in a hostile country in which I couldn't understand a word of the language. I suddenly appreciated how heavily I'd been leaning on Vera's shoulders.

The sun was still an eye-searing bronze disk in the western sky when she suggested that since it was our last night in Russia together, perhaps we should celebrate.

"I wish I felt more like it," I observed gloomily.

"Well, then let's go drown our sorrows," she went on brightly.

"That would be more in keeping with this overheated, seaside garbage dump."

She gazed at me and her eyes were suddenly somber. "Why don't you come with me tomorrow?"

"Don't tempt me."

"If I begged you?"

"Thank God, you're not the type."

"And if I say I won't go unless you come, too?"

"Don't complicate things at this final hour. You know I won't leave until I've at least tried to get him out. And you must realize that I'm only asking you to leave because there is nothing more you can do to help. You've been absolutely magnificent and without you I wouldn't have gotten this close to Englhardt in a thousand years." I paused and stared down at my hands. "But you must go now. Your presence will only hinder us if we have to make a run for it." I glanced up at her, "You see I'm being perfectly frank."

"Quite a speech," she said calmly. "But do you understand why I have helped you?"

"I think so. I hope so."

"I wonder."

For a long time I stared at her, but her expression completely baffled me. As it had happened so often before, it seemed as though suddenly there was no contact between us, absolutely none. Even the physical ties which had bound us together seemed to have broken. I asked myself if we two were fated to spend our lives together, climbing the heights of exquisite pleasure only to drop back into the valleys of cold indifference.

We had dinner at an outdoor restaurant by the shore and watched a fabulous sunset and drank far too much vodka. We talked of inconsequentialities, each of us withdrawn behind a protective, impersonal screen. Whether it was the apprehension, the fear of the immediate future, or the morbid mood encouraged by the vodka, I didn't know. But I had a gnawing premonition deep down inside me that when she left tomorrow, I would never see her again.

It was late when we walked up to the shop in the alleyway. A dim light shone through from the passage in the rear, and the door was unlocked. Carefully, we threaded our way through the crates of overripe-smelling vegetables littering the floor and I knocked on the counter. A moment later the henna-haired madame, stuffed into a tawdry, flowered silk evening dress that emphasized every curve and wrinkle, floated in on a wave of cheap-smelling perfume. And from somewhere down the hall, a phonograph began to grind out a scratchy record.

No, she said, there was no message. But as the parcel had only gone that morning, there was hardly time.

Vera said that I would return in a day or two.

And that would be fine, she said, staring at me, her black eyes full of invitation.

Suppressing a sudden, insane desire to laugh, I stumbled out into the night.

"What's the matter?" Vera demanded when she'd caught up to me.

"I don't know. I guess I'm a little drunk. But the atmosphere in there is so incredibly, unbelievably corny. God! Even a phonograph!"

"You are drunk!" she said severely.

"Okay," I said, putting my around her, "take me home to the Ritz."

We left Kerch at dawn and even the taxi driver was amazed that we made Sevastopol with only one blowout. We had time for a quick swim and dinner before the plane left. There was the usual routine police inspection at the airport, and then there was nothing left but to say goodbye.

"I'll go directly to my mother in Paris," she said. "And you know I'll be worrying."

"I'll cable you as soon as I can," I promised. "Keep your fingers crossed." I grinned at her and tried to swallow the lump that was choking me.

She brushed my cheek with her lips. "Goodbye, Sir Galahad," she whispered and disappeared into the plane.

CHAPTER ELEVEN

I HAD ARRANGED with the taxi driver to stay overnight in Sevastopol and take me back to Kerch the next day. But on the return journey we weren't so lucky. We blew a tire before reaching Simferopol, another near Belogorsk and it was after midnight when we finally limped into Kerch. I had taken advantage of the lengthy delays while the tires were being repaired in various towns to purchase a stock of food. I bought only tinned or bottled products, items that would keep indefinitely, and I concentrated on energy-building meats and pastes.

The manager was still up when I reached the hotel. I signed the customary police form, gave him my passport and after explaining that I was going out for a drink asked him not to lock me out.

I hurried up to the shop in the alleyway but the door was locked and there were no lights showing. I started by tapping the glass with my ring and ended by pounding the door with my fist. Eventually a light glowed and a moment later the woman appeared clutching a negligee around her and stared through the glass panel of the door. When she recognized me, she unlocked the door and I slipped inside. She said good evening in broken German, and I wondered if Vera had said I was a German, or whether, realizing I was a foreigner, she was using the only foreign language she knew.

After apologizing for disturbing her at this late hour, I asked if there was any message from the camp. Without answering, she took my arm and guided me towards the passageway. When I felt the pressure of her hand, I began to suspect that if Englhardt did send an answer, it was going to cost me more money to get it out of this blowsy harridan.

She opened a door off the passage, switched on a bright lamp and ushered me into a small living room overstuffed with battered, gold-plush furniture. She closed the door and invited me to sit down. There were no windows and the atmosphere was heavy with the smell of stale tobacco smoke, cheap perfume and human bodies. In one corner stood a very elaborate victrola, circa 1925, and for a dreadful moment, I was afraid she was going to put on a record.

"You speak German very well," I observed, sitting on the edge of a chair.

"I should," she replied with a dry laugh. "The bastards were here for four years. What would you like to drink?"

"Vodka would be fine."

"You wouldn't prefer schnapps?"

I wouldn't, but since she apparently mistook me for a German, I said, "Of course. But I didn't think you'd have any."

She unlocked a cabinet. Deciding I'd have to play it her way, I leaned back in the chair and studied her. If it hadn't been for the atrocious shade she'd dyed her hair, her face was not unpleasant. She wore little make-up; only her mouth, well-shaped with a full lower lip, was heavily rouged. Her cheeks were pale, inclined to be fleshy and looked as though they hadn't been near sunlight for years. Her eyes were coal black, Georgian, and were the most brazen eyes I'd ever seen. The negligee covering her heavy body was reasonably clean, certainly imported from one of the more frivolous countries, and it was obvious that it was all she had on. Her bare feet were tucked into dilapidated Turkish slippers with up-curving toes and her ankles were surprisingly trim. There was little subtlety to the perfume she must have doused herself with when she'd heard the knock on the door.

She took a tall-necked bottle and two small glasses out of the cabinet, set the glasses on a low Oriental table in front of the couch and filled them. "You'll find it more comfortable here," she said, indicating the couch.

I moved over and sat in a corner. She picked up a glass, sat down in the other corner of the couch and crossed her legs. And as far as it still covered her body, she might as well have taken the negligee off. I sipped the schnapps and cursed myself for not waiting until the morning to come for Englhardt's answer.

"You manage to live well," I said, indicating the bottle. "Black market?"

"There are always ways and means—if you have the money."

"And living in a seaport must help."

"It's not like the old days. About the only ships we get through here now are coal barges from Rostov to Odessa."

I set the glass down slowly and got out a package of cigarettes. I let the idea that had suddenly hit me sink in. I offered her a cigarette.

"American?" she said, taking one and glancing at it.

"I bought them in Berlin. But I don't mind yours. In fact your tobacco and vodka are two things I've acquired a taste for."

She let the smoke curl out of her nostrils. "And our women? That was a nice piece you had with you. Where did you pick her up, Moscow?"

I laughed. "You've got the wrong impression. She was my interpreter."

"Is that her boyfriend, the man in the prison camp she sent the parcel to?" She didn't use the word boyfriend.

"Yes, and by the way, have you heard from him?"

She took another puff of the cigarette and while her sensuous eyes undressed me, slowly exhaled. "You Germans are always impatient."

"It's late and I don't want to keep you up."

"Relax." She chuckled. "And pour yourself another drink."

"You live alone here?"

"With Olga, my daughter. But it's been quiet tonight and she's gone to bed."

"How old is she?"

"Fifteen."

"You've got a nice place. The police don't, ah, bother you?"

"Why should they?" Her lips curled contemptuously. "They know that if we didn't entertain those young bloods from the camp once in a while, they'd be out raping *their* daughters."

"That's one way of looking at it," I said, suppressing a slight shudder. I picked up the bottle and refilled the glasses. "How do you get this stuff?" I had pushed Englhardt's message into the back of my mind for the moment, and was concentrating on the last stage of the escape route. For I'd sensed the moment I'd seen that bottle of schnapps that if there was anyone in the port who might know a smuggler, it was this woman sitting beside me. And a smuggler would know about ships...

But all she said was, "I've got friends."

I leaned towards her; fortunately the perfume was wearing off—or I was getting used to it. "Is there much smuggling going on down here?"

Her expression abruptly sharpened and an agate-hard glint crept into her black eyes. "I wouldn't know anything about it."

"Oh, come now," I laughed easily. "A gal as smart as you must know what goes on in this town."

"And so?"

"It appears to me there'd be a big market here." I leaned back. "You get a lot of vacationers down from the north and they must have money to spend on liquor, silk stockings, perfume—you know, whatever they can't get at home."

Her eyes were still watching me but she made no comment.

"And it so happens," I went on, confidentially, "that I spend a great deal of time in Istanbul. Perhaps you and I might work out some sort of a deal."

Slowly she turned away from me and stared at the glowing end of her cigarette. Then with a tremendous sense of relief, I noticed her unconsciously draw the negligee across her enormous breasts and I knew that avariciousness had driven sex out of her mind.

"I've a friend I might talk to," she said quietly.

"Has he got a boat?" I held my breath waiting for her answer.

But she was exasperatingly noncommittal. "There are always boats," she said.

Once again I filled the glasses. "Well," I said clicking my glass against hers, "here's to you and me and your friend making a fortune." I knocked the drink back and sat up. "And now I'd better go or I'll find the hotel locked up."

"Oh, you can stay here," she said casually. "I like you."

"And I like you. But I'm a foreigner and these damn police of yours know every time I go to the bathroom. And if we're going into business together, I don't think we should advertise the fact that we're too friendly." I stood up and put my hand on my wallet. "Let me pay for the drinks."

She waved a work-stained, heavily ringed hand. "Forget it. I said I liked you." But she continued to sit there and I wondered how I was going to get out of the place.

"Try and talk to your friend tomorrow and I'll come back tomorrow night," I said. "But don't waste time. My permit expires in a few days."

Eventually she stood up. "Don't come too early or you might find the place crowded."

She followed me out into the passage. But instead of turning towards the shop, she turned in the opposite direction and at the end of the hall, drew back a bolt and opened a door. Like a man with an eleventh-hour reprieve from a death sentence, I gulped down the cool clean night air.

"I was forgetting what I came for," I said, pausing on the step. "The note."

"Oh, that." She dismissed it with a wave of her hand. "I'll give it to you tomorrow. But his girlfriend is going to be disappointed."

"Yes?"

"He didn't even bother to say thinks. All he said was *da*." She shrugged her heavy shoulders. "What did she ask him? If he was being faithful to her?"

The burst of raucous laughter followed me out into the night.

The next day was Friday and Sunday night would be the seventh night, the night I'd told Englhardt to be ready. Fortunately I had given myself some leeway; I'd said to be prepared from the seventh night onwards. But for two reasons I wanted to make the attempt Sunday night. The first was that I had no idea of the routine or regulations within the camp and it was quite possible that the convicts were locked in their shacks at night or some other precautions taken, and he would have to arrange to get outside. And the second reason was that I was becoming very nervous hanging around Kerch. The police hadn't bothered me again, but they knew I'd returned from Sevastopol. The hotel manager would have reported it. And as they had so rightly pointed out, Kerch was about the last place a foreigner would choose to vacation in on the Crimea. And if they didn't already, they soon would suspect that I was here for some other reason.

I spent Friday cycling along the highway inland. I'd already travelled that road several times, but I wanted to memorize every bump and pothole. About eight miles from Kerch a narrow dirt track branched off towards the south, petering out a mile farther in the scrub-covered, craggy hills that led down to the coast. It was desolate, almost impassable country and I chose this spot for our first day. They'd need dogs to route us out and although I wasn't completely certain, I was pretty sure no dog could follow the scent of a bicycle tire for eight miles. The second day I planned to be on the other side of Feodosiya. It meant a forty mile night ride, but once we reached those rugged coastal mountains, I figured they would require the army as well as the air force to find us. And since Englhardt was considered a common criminal and not a dangerous political agitator, I was counting on his escape being treated solely as a local police matter. Once in the mountains we could hole up if necessary for a week and, when the heat was off, find a boat. I rode back to Kerch full of confidence.

It was just after midnight when I knocked on the door of the shop. There was a light on inside, but it was not until the woman opened the door that I heard the racket from down the passage. The victrola was playing and from the loud conversation and bursts of laughter, some of the boys were having a night out. She was wearing the flowered silk evening dress and from the glazed look in her black eyes, I gathered that she had been keeping up with her guests.

I told her I'd come back later, but she insisted it was all right, and closed the door behind me. Instead of taking me down to the gold room, she led me up a flight of steep, narrow steps, opened a door and switched on a light. It was a tiny, cell-like room and most of the floor space was taken up with a wide bed. In one corner was a washstand and underneath a bucket and that was all the furniture the room contained. There were no windows and no covering on the dirty slate-colored straw mattress. From the acrid smell in the air, the bucket needed emptying badly.

"Wait here," she said, her hand on my arm, "until I can get rid of them. I'll send you up a drink."

I swallowed the protest that had leaped to my lips and reminded myself that Englhardt would consider this odious cubby hole the bridal suite by now. I sat down on the edge of the bed and lit a cigarette.

The door opened a few minutes later and a young, well-built brunette entered carrying a bottle of vodka and a glass. I presumed she was Olga, the daughter. If she was only fifteen she had ripened fast, and from the expression in her hazel eyes, she had ripened early. She was wearing the conventional costume for such establishments, but her eye for color and style was better than her mother's. The evening dress fitted her and didn't look as though it had been whipped up out of an old bedspread.

I said good evening in German, but she shrugged and gave me a vacant smile and I gathered her education so far as languages were concerned was not so extensive as her mother's. She handed me the glass and I held it while she filled it. I knocked the drink back. She sat down on the bed beside me and refilled the glass. I sipped the second drink slowly. The first had tasted like kerosene, and the rueful thought passed through my mind that my credit in this off-beat bordello must have slipped. The first night it had been imported schnapps. Now it was fourth grade vodka.

She smiled at me and I smiled back and wondered if she'd been sent up to help me pass the time. I tried my few words of Russian, but they came with difficulty, and I began to wish there was some way of getting fresh air into the room. I set the glass on the floor and loosened my collar and decided that I'd cycled too far that day. I was tired, dead tired; much too tired to cope with all these problems...

The last thing I remember before passing out was the firm grip of her hands on my ankles as she shifted my feet onto the bed.

They were beating my head with a sledgehammer, so I woke up to tell them to stop. But the hammer was my heart pumping the blood into my drugged brain. I tried to swallow some of the fur that filled my mouth but my throat rasped. I rolled over and staggered to my feet and fumbled at the door handle. It was locked. I sat down on the bed again and held my head and let my senses gradually sort themselves out.

I had been mickey-finned. That was about the only thing I was sure of. But why? Slowly, painfully, I went through my pockets. They were empty—travellers' checks, cash, even my cigarettes and lighter had disappeared. Thank God, I told myself, the hotel manager hadn't returned my passport from the last time I'd checked in. And at that moment it was all I cared for. A passport to get out of this bloody country by the first available means. To hell with Englhardt, to hell with everybody. Sir Galahad was throwing away his wooden sword. I wallowed through a bog of self-pity.

And then I got mad. I stood up and pounded the door. By God! I'd get the police and then we'd see how fast that henna-haired bitch could talk! I stood back and kicked the door panel. But the wood was solid. I picked up the washstand, and heard the key turning in the lock.

The door pushed open and a man entered. He closed the door behind him and leaned up against it. "Take it easy, chum," he said. "Can't have you breaking up the place."

I stared at him, my mouth open with amazement, and slowly set down the washstand. He had spoken in English with a pronounced Cockney accent.

And then my anger flared again. "Let me out of here!" I cried, starting towards him. He was slender and middle-aged, but even if he'd been a hulking gorilla, at that moment I would have taken him on.

"Now, now, chum," he cautioned, his voice calm. I heard a brittle click and caught the glint of a naked blade in his right hand. "Why don't we sit down and talk things over like gentlemen?"

I stopped and glared at him. And then I sat down. Not because he'd suggested it, but because a sudden wave of nausea swam over me and I was afraid I was going to be physically sick.

"You don't look so good," he said. "Do you want a drink?"

"Yes," I muttered holding my head. "Water."

He opened the door and called out—in Russian. A few moments later someone handed him a bottle. He closed the door and passed the bottle to me. I tipped it up and gulped down the flat, tepid liquid.

"One day that old bitch is going to kill somebody with her knock-out drops," he said, not unkindly. "Want a cigarette?"

"No." I wiped my lips with the back of my hand and set the bottle down on the floor. The nausea faded and as I glanced up at this rat-faced individual with the Bow Bells accent, I felt fear. There was something going on here besides robbery. "What's the game?" I said.

Slowly, he closed the blade of the knife. "Well, chum, perhaps you'd better tell us what your game is first."

"I'm not playing any game. I came up here to talk to this woman and she gives me a mickey finn and rolls me. Okay, so it's a clip joint. Now can I go?"

He showed a mouthful of tobacco-stained, broken teeth. "All in good time. But if you're not up to something, why did you tell Tanya you're a German when everybody else in the port knows you're an American?"

"I never told her I was a German. She assumed it because it was the only common language we had."

"I see. And if you only came here to have a drink and perhaps a little fun with her daughter, why were you talking about contraband?"

My brain was clearing now and I was beginning to think straight. "Who are you anyway, her husband?"

"She hasn't got one. I'm just a friend."

"A friend from the police?" I was pretty sure he wasn't. I doubted whether the Soviet secret police were scraping that far down in the barrel. But where did he acquire that knowledge of English?

He spat on the floor. "Do I look like a copper?"

"Where did you learn to speak English?"

He shifted uneasily. "Look, chum—I came up here to ask questions, not to answer them. Now let's try again. What'd you come here for?"

"You should have asked me that before you spiked my drink. I might have told you."

"You're too well built and Tanya can't afford to have a rough house here."

"And if I start one now?"

"I don't think you will, chum." There was a steely glint in his dark eyes. "Besides, we wanted to look over your credentials."

"Now that you have, how about returning them?"

"As I said before, all in good time. You an American secret agent?"

"Don't be a bloody fool. Would I be hanging around a joint like this if I was?"

He shrugged. "You'd hardly be hanging around the police bureau."

"I grant you the point. No, I'm not a spy. I'm just an ordinary tourist that was stupid enough to visit your godforsaken country."

He showed his teeth again, and I gathered it was his way of smiling. "We're going to be here all day if you keep stalling like this."

And like a hammer, the thought struck me that I not only didn't know what time it was, I didn't know what day it was. If it was already Sunday... "What's the time?" I asked.

"About noon. Why? You hungry?"

"Saturday?"

"Of course. You just had a good night's sleep."

"Sure, and if I didn't have a splitting headache and a mouth that tastes like the inside of your boot I might believe you." I hunched forward. "Look, whatever your name is, I'm not only hungry but I'm fed up with this stinking hole and the rats in it. So what do I have to tell you before I can get out?"

A flush of anger showed through the gray stubble covering his lined, weather-beaten cheeks. "Maybe I should take you down to the cellar and work you over a bit."

"Put that knife away and we'll soon see who works whom over."

"Tough guy, eh?" With a click the blade appeared again. "I think I'll see how tough you are right here."

"Oh, put that pig-sticker away," I said, tired of the whole business. This argument was not only futile, but a complete waste of time. I had plenty of things to do before tomorrow night, and if he wasn't going to release me until I gave him a story, the sooner I satisfied his curiosity, the better. Provided they returned the travellers' checks, they could keep everything else. I had no intention of reporting them to the police. The first question they'd ask was what was I doing here. But I had to have those checks; without that little blue folder we'd have to swim across the Black Sea. "If the offer still holds," I said, "I'd like a cigarette now."

He brought out a package of Turkish cigarettes, flipped one out and handed it to me. Instinctively I reached for my lighter. I dropped my hand and gave him a wry grin. "Guess you'll have to give me a light too," I said. "The only thing I'm left with is the desire." Without comment he handed me a box of matches.

I leaned back against the iron bedpost and inhaled the sweet tobacco smoke. "All right, if you want the truth, I came around here looking for a man with a boat to take me across to Turkey. All that talk about contraband was only a build-up. I figured the dame who runs this joint must have some friends on the waterfront and perhaps she could find someone who could help me."

Interest had replaced anger now and, although his expression was highly speculative, I felt that he didn't completely disbelieve me. "Why do you have to sneak out of the country?" he asked. "You hot or something?"

"Yes and no," I answered confidentially. "I haven't committed any crime, if that's what you mean. But I've been hanging around with a girl who has made the police suspicious. She got out of the country a couple of days ago before they could do anything about it. But I have a feeling that when I try to leave, they're going to arrest me."

"Is she the dame with the boyfriend out at the prison camp?"

"So you know about that?"

"I'm asking, not answering."

"Yes, it's the same woman."

A shrewd look crept into his eyes and for a fearful moment I was afraid I'd said too much; that I'd supplied him with the link which connected the man in the prison camp with a boat.

"Try again, chum," he muttered, his thin lips curling. "That dame was a Frenchwoman. At least she was travelling on a French passport. How come she's got a boyfriend in the local convict camp?"

I explained at some length that the prisoner had been working in Belgium for the Soviet Government and that was where they'd met. In fact, I went on, that was why he'd been arrested. He'd been caught embezzling government funds to spend on her.

"Is that why the police are suspicious of her?"

"No, at least I don't think so. They don't know anything about that angle unless you or the woman here told them."

Again he spat. It seemed as though every time he mentioned the word police he had to clear the taste out of his mouth.

"They're suspicious," I went on, "because she's been hanging around the Soviet Youth Club. She speaks Russian and she hates Communism and I guess she'd been broadcasting the fact." It was a weak story, but it was the best I could think up at the moment and there was enough truth in it, I hoped, to make it sound convincing. I didn't consider him a mental heavyweight and I was relying a great deal on the inbred fear they all had of the political police.

"And she got away. How?"

"By plane."

"And you think they'll nab you when you try to follow?"

"That's what I don't know." I shrugged. "If they're annoyed because she slipped away, they might decide to take it out on me."

"Beria's dead, chum. Didn't you know? Everybody gets a fair shake now in Russia. And if you've done nothing wrong—"

The epithet I voiced was understandable, I think, even in Russian.

He laughed. "So you want to slip out with no questions asked." And while he slowly rubbed his unshaven jaw with his knuckles, his brow lowered in thought, the idea finally got through to my sluggish brain that perhaps this little rat might be able to help me. I explored the idea further and my hopes began Jo build. Perhaps that's why he was so inquisitive. Perhaps he was a smuggler—an intimate of the woman whom she'd tipped off. And he and the woman had decided in their own peculiar fashion to find out first who I really was and why I was interested in contraband before they discussed it with me. He'd spent many years abroad, or working in foreign ships. His English proved that. And he was smoking black market cigarettes.

My confidence increasing, I toyed with the idea of revealing the whole, true story about Englhardt and how I was planning to free him and why I needed the boat. We could have worked out definite times and places which would have eliminated the dangerous delay hiding out in the mountains. He might, with his knowledge of the pipe line into the prison camp, even be able to suggest an easier, safer method of getting Englhardt out.

But there was something about his expression and the shifty look in his beady eyes that checked me. Smuggling a frightened foreigner out of the country was one thing. An escaped convict, a Russian national, might be an entirely different story. And if he refused to have anything to do with it, I was ready to bet double the money I'd lost last night that he'd sell my story to someone, even if it had to be the spit-provoking police. I decided that the time to tell him there would be two of us would be the moment, if it ever arrived, when we both stepped on board.

"You know someone who might help me?" I asked.

"I don't know," he replied reflectively. "But if I did it would cost you a lot of money."

"It would be worth it—if I got out safely."

He straightened up and I gathered the interview was over.

"Speaking of money," I said, "how about asking that dame downstairs to return mine?"

Dropping the knife into his pocket, he took my wallet out and tossed it on the bed. I picked it up and glanced through it. The folder of travellers' checks was there—apparently they were intelligent enough to realize they weren't any good without my signature—but the roubles were missing.

"No cash?" I said drily, glancing up at him.

"You got to pay for the room," he smirked.

"Quite an expensive hotel you're running here." But I wasn't going to make an issue of fifty dollars worth of local currency at this stage of the game. I put the wallet into my pocket. "When do I see you again?"

"I'll get in touch with you in a few days."

"Few days, hell!" I stood up. "I want to leave now—tomorrow or the next day."

"You can't rush these things." And I knew from the whine in his voice that he'd produce a boat.

"Look," I said, "you've got an opportunity to make more money than you've ever made at one time in your life. But I've got to know by noon tomorrow whether you're smart enough to make it. Otherwise, I'm going over to Sevastopol and see if I can't find a more intelligent boatman."

He let me out through the back entrance. I didn't run into the mother or daughter. It was probably just as well. My limited supply of sulphurous German words would not have been adequate.

When I arrived back at the hotel, the manager returned my passport and handed me a cable from Vera. The first thing I glanced at was the date line. It had been sent from Paris and a tremendous weight slid off my shoulders. She was safe. The message must have baffled the censors. For a time it even baffled me. *I prefer a live Quixote to a dead Galahad* was all it said.

CHAPTER TWELVE

KEPT OUT of sight for the rest of that day and night. My head felt as though it had been run over by a tank and I wanted no questions by inquisitive policemen nor doped drinks from fifteen year old females. If the Rat—I considered that name more fitting than any his mother could have given him—wanted me, he knew where I was staying.

Sunday morning dawned cold and clear and I woke up shivering with apprehension. I spent the morning sorting out my gear. The food more than filled the pack and it was much too heavy for my liking. But there would be two of us to feed and I had no idea for how long. With the exception of the clothes I was wearing, I packed everything else in the suitcase and kissed it goodbye. I couldn't take it with me, and it was not very likely the authorities would forward it on afterwards.

The Rat turned up at noon, as I had expected he would. Whether he believed my story or not, he knew I had money. And it would have surprised me if he hadn't appeared with a proposition to relieve me of some or all of it. He kept glancing over his shoulder while talking to me and finally I suggested we find a more discreet place than the hotel. He described a café on the waterfront and slid out of sight.

He was waiting inside when I eventually found the café, and asked me what I'd have to drink. I grinned at him and said nothing, thanks, that on Sundays I didn't indulge. He said he'd found a fishing boat that would take me across to Sinop on Tuesday night if the weather was suitable. I didn't know where Sinop was, but since it was presumably in Turkey, it wasn't important. Then I put the dollar question and he said seven thousand. I sat back and laughed in his face. There'd been exactly seven thousand one hundred and fifty dollars left in that book of travellers' checks.

"I may be worried," I said, "but I'm not that worried about getting out of here."

He lowered his narrow shoulders and lifted his hands. "But if I'm caught they'll give me twenty years."

"It's been nice knowing you." I pushed back my chair.

"Wait a minute. What do you figure it's worth?"

I figured it would be worth every cent of seven thousand dollars to watch Englhardt step ashore in Turkey. But I wasn't going to admit that to him. If he knew I was willing to pay that much he would get ideas. And halfway across, or even before we set out, the fare might increase tenfold.

I told him I'd give him five hundred now, five hundred when I stepped on board and five hundred when we reached the other side. This time he leaned back and laughed and suggested I go to Sevastopol.

Fifteen minutes later we agreed on a price of twenty-four hundred dollars; a third now, a third when I came aboard and the remainder when I landed.

Then, after explaining that I'd have to come aboard outside the strait as it was often patrolled, he asked me if I knew the coast. I said no, and he took a folded, oil-stained map from inside his jacket and spread it out on the table.

"There's a deep cove between these two capes," he said, indicating with a grimy finger a point about midway between Kerch and Feodosiya. "It's just off one of the fishing grounds. Be on the beach at the top of this cove on Tuesday night and we'll pick you up in the dory."

"What time?"

He thought for a moment. "The moon sets after two that night." Yes, I reminded myself, and tonight it sets before one. "You'd better be there from midnight on," he finished.

"Can I get there by road?"

"You'll have to walk the last few miles down to the coast. The path's marked on this map." He refolded the map and handed it to me. "Give this back to me on Tuesday."

"How do you want the money? Roubles?"

"No, just sign some of those checks."

"But they won't cash them for you without my passport."

"I'll worry about that. When will we meet again?"

I took out my wallet. "We won't—until Tuesday night." I endorsed eight one-hundred-dollar checks and pushed them across the table. "I'm leaving this town today. I'll probably stay in Feodosiya. They don't know me over there." I stood up. "And if for some reason you don't turn up on Tuesday?"

"If the weather's bad, I'll come Wednesday or the first night it's calm."

Walking back to the hotel I had an uncomfortable feeling that I'd just tossed away eight hundred dollars. But the feeling didn't last long. It was soon replaced by the disconcerting realization of how naive I was in this cloak and dagger game. I'd neglected to find out where he lived in case I had to alter my plans. In fact, I hadn't even asked him his name!

Late that afternoon I rode one of the bicycles down to the Intourist office—Sunday is just another business day in the Soviet week—and bought two thousand roubles. I cycled out the highway and a couple of miles from the outskirts of the port, turned off the road, lay down in a meadow and tried to go to sleep. But I was far too excited, or nervous, and it seemed as though a century of time passed before the flaming red sun touched the western horizon. Off in the distance were the silhouettes of the slag heaps, and I wondered if Nicholas Englhardt was also impatiently watching that sunset, asking himself where he'd be when it rose again.

The short twilight was giving way to night when I cycled along the narrow lane connecting the highway with the camp road. There were no street lamps this far out, and by the time I'd reached the clump of bushes I'd previously chosen, visibility was down to a few hundred yards. I shoved the bicycle into the bushes, and returned to the hotel at a fast walk.

I'd already paid the bill and checked out and explained to the manager that I was cycling by easy stages to Sevastopol. He wasn't surprised or very interested; it was the way most of the Soviet youth toured this motorless country. I'd also asked him to ship my suitcase on by boat. It might prove a small red herring if the police came around asking questions later.

Unfortunately, I ran into him at the entrance. I gave him a story about how it had taken all afternoon to sell the other bicycle. He glanced up at the sky, shrugged and said it was a good night to sleep out, but it might be cold. At that moment I hoped it would be. My shirt was sticking to my back.

I fastened the heavy pack to the rear of the other bicycle, said goodbye again, and headed westward.

By half past one the moon had set and despite the star-studded canopy above, the road was a pale, featureless patch of gray that disappeared a few feet in front of the handlebars as I cycled towards the camp. The shapes of bushes and trees seemed to have altered with the darkness and it was with some difficulty I located the other bicycle.

The searchlights were ablaze around the camp. I saw no sign of movement, but I was sure that in the shadows by the gate and in those watch towers, sharp-eyed men were staring out into the night. And as I drew nearer I muttered to myself that the pole carrying the power lines I had selected was too close. I was afraid to admit the truth—that my stomach was taut with undiluted fear and that my chicken heart was thundering in my ears.

I laid the bicycles in the ditch and risked the flare of a match to look at my watch. It was eight minutes to two. I removed my jacket, checked the pliers in my back pocket and retied the tennis shoes I was wearing. The night was deathly still and only the nervous bark of a dog back toward the port broke the heavy silence. I crouched over another match. Four minutes had passed. I caught hold of the thick pole, pulled myself up, locked my legs around it and pulled again.

Halfway up, the sweat was blinding me and this time it wasn't from fright. Two thirds of the way, I hung there for one awful minute and wondered if I could make it. My arms and hands were numb and there was little feeling left in my bruised legs.

And then I got an arm over the crossbar and choked down the bloody gorge in my mouth. But it was a long time before I could steady my trembling hands and I knew if I dropped the pliers now...

With a soft snick the heavy cutters bit through the first cable and it snapped back into the night. I glanced towards the camp. There wasn't a pinpoint of light to be seen anywhere. I cut the second cable, slipped the pliers into my pocket, and slid down the pole. I put on my jacket, leaned a bicycle against the pole as a marker, and ran across the fields toward the fence.

I saw Englhardt when he was still on the other side of the wire. Snatching out my pliers, I helped him cut out a hole. A moment later he was beside me, and I felt his powerful hand grip mine. Without a word, I turned and raced towards the bicycles and I could hear him panting at my shoulder.

They were shouting now inside the camp and here and there a flashlight flared. But the road was still deserted as we leapt on the bicycles and headed toward the port. I let him get ahead and from my pocket scattered handfuls of the roofing nails on the roadway behind us. We were abreast the turnoff before I spotted it and I had to call him back.

We reached the highway and turned westward and still there was no sign of pursuit. Every so often I scattered more nails and finally they were gone. I was reasonably sure puncture-proof tires were not yet in use in Russia and although I was leaving a trail which might be spotted by daylight, it was a calculated risk I had to take. I could think of no other way to slow up the cars or motorcycles which might be sent out in pursuit. When my pockets were empty, I took the lead, settled down to a fast, steady pace and tried to recall the bad patches on the road. The side route to the coast came up sooner than I'd expected and I wished I'd chosen one farther on. We turned off and rode down towards the coast until the narrow, stoney path made it impossible, got down and walked, pushing our bicycles beside us.

And it was not until then that Englhardt spoke.

"I knew you would come," he said quietly. "But I had no way of stopping you."

"I'm glad it wasn't Siberia." I stumbled through a thick bush that had overgrown the path. "But as you can see," I cracked lamely, "we're not out of the woods yet."

After we had reached a fairly clear stretch, he said, "Where is the girl?"

"Returned to Paris. How did you know she was here?"

"The guard described the woman who sent the food parcel. It could only have been her."

For some minutes we walked along in silence. Then I asked him, "What else do you know about her?"

"If you mean do I know she turned me in—yes, of course."

"What happened that weekend in Spa?"

"Are you in love with her?" he countered.

"That's a difficult question to answer," I said hesitatingly. "When—"

"Then you're not." He chuckled quietly to himself. "I wish I'd known that in Spa. We wouldn't be pushing bicycles through the Crimean underbrush now."

"In other words, you were protecting my interests? What made you think I was in love with her? Did she tell you?"

"No. But you don't spend weekends with someone you're not interested in."

"She tell you about the weekends?"

"No."

"I keep forgetting how close you play the game," I said drily. "So you'd been watching us."

"Naturally. When I discovered the secretary of the company was a White Russian—and an extremely attractive one —I was afraid you might do something foolish that would get us into trouble."

"Instead of which, you did something foolish."

"I was anxious to find out her feelings for you."

"And when she indicated she didn't have many, you spanked her and packed her off home. Which might not have been so bad if you hadn't been, as far as she knew, a Communist. I can appreciate how that must have burned her up ! What else did you do, give her a little fatherly advice on how young Russian ladies behaved today?"

"Perhaps I did say a few things ..."

His voice drifted off and I exploded with a "Good God!" Despite the seriousness of the results, I couldn't suppress a snort of laughter when I visualized Vera sitting on the edge of a bed with perhaps only the smoke of her cigarette clothing her, being told the facts of life by a petty Soviet *fonctionnaire.*

"It's a wonder," I said, "that she didn't cut your throat with your own razor. Particularly since you'd created some sort of precedent."

"You mean—?"

"You, my friend, are the first man who didn't succumb to her charms."

"You sound bitter."

"I guess I am in a way. But don't misunderstand me. I'm bitter because of the life that was forced upon her, that made her adopt the attitude she has towards us, towards all men."

"Which is why you're afraid to let yourself fall in love with her. You're afraid you couldn't live with her past."

I glanced back at him but in the darkness his face was completely expressionless. "Well, whatever she has done to you," I said, "she has more than made up for. Without her help you'd still be chipping ore and I'd undoubtedly be helping you."

"She is very Russian," he said and again I heard that quiet, provocative laughter. "And very persistent when she wants something."

I was about to ask him just exactly what he meant, when I crashed into a low-hanging bough. By the time I had extricated myself and found the path again, I'd lost interest in anyone but myself. My legs ached, my face was a burning griddle of scratches and I was completely exhausted from the mental as well as the physical strain of that night. "Whatever she is," I mumbled bitterly, "I wish to hell we were where she is right now!"

The dawn was washing the eastern sky with silver when we struggled up the last craggy slope. I flopped down against a rocky shoulder and rested my head on my arms.

"Is this as far as we go?" he said, surveying the country around us.

"Yes," I panted. "And I was beginning to be afraid we'd never get this far."

He eased the pack off his shoulders and set it on the ground. He'd insisted on carrying it ever since we'd hidden our bicycles below. "You're out of condition," he said with his quick laugh. "You should spend some time in an iron mine." He stretched out on a patch of turf beside me and went to sleep.

We spent that day hiding in the shelter of a ledge of rock overlooking the eastern tip of the peninsula. We couldn't see the highway, but from time to time a ribbon of dust would unravel beyond a distant ridge of trees indicating the passage of some vehicle. But whether it was searching for us or just part of the usual traffic, we had no way of knowing. None stopped, and as far as we could judge, none turned into the side road.

I explained how I had met the Rat and had arranged for him to come and pick us up off the beach, and added that it wouldn't surprise me if he didn't appear. If that happened, we would lay low for a few days in the mountains and then search for another ship to take us across to Turkey. I asked him if he knew the country and he said no, but after questioning me for some time about the Rat, he seemed to think he would show up. I sincerely hoped so. If he did, I would double the fare.

Before the shadows of night had closed in, we descended, picked up the bicycles and returned to the highway. I had memorized the map the Rat had given me and I knew that the road which turned off the highway and which eventually became the path to the cove was eighteen miles farther west. But my conception of distance from a bicycle seat was extremely limited and I asked Englhardt if his was any better. He admitted it wasn't, so after midnight we kept an eye trained on the left side of the highway. We turned down two roads before we discovered the one that curved according to the map, and the golden edge of the sun was showing above the tree-tipped horizon by the time we saw the sea. The path we were following looked well-travelled, and I suggested finding a hideout before we ran into anyone. Dragging the bicycles, we crawled into a thicket. When I stretched out on the stony ground, I'd have given a lot for even the odorous bed in henna-haired Tanya's bordello.

Long before midnight that night, we descended to the cove. After carefully checking the contours of the coast against the map, there wasn't the slightest doubt in my mind that we were on the right beach. But midnight came and went, and the rose-colored moon dipped below the flat, oily surface of the sea and still there was no sound of an engine.

At three o'clock I told Englhardt I was afraid the Rat wasn't coming. At four o'clock, I was sure of it. And when we could discern the nearest headland in detail, I said that we'd better move off the beach and find another hideout.

Recovering our bicycles, we rode inland about a mile and crawled into a brambly thicket well off the path. While Englhardt surveyed the diminishing stock of food, I lay down on the ground and let my spirits nose-dive. The escape from the prison camp had been so simple—I'd long since forgotten the sick-making fear of that night—that I'd contemplated the rest of the journey to freedom with buoyant hopes. I overlooked the fact that we were, right now, in the exact position I'd counted on being before meeting the Rat.

Englhardt opened a can of beef and cut several thick slices of hard brown bread. "Cheer up," he said brightly, handing me a sandwich. "Perhaps his engine broke down."

Gloomily, I shook my head. "You don't know that character. I had the feeling when I paid him that I would never see him again."

"In that case, it's just as well you didn't pay him any more. But I think we should give him another night."

We did. But when dawn had turned the color of the sea from black to gunmetal, even Englhardt admitted that there was no use in waiting any longer.

CHAPTER THIRTEEN

THE NEXT DAY WAS one thousand hours long. We'd recovered from our cross-country bicycle race Sunday night and although neither of us felt like sleeping, we realized it would be foolish to show ourselves on the highway before dark. The sea, mirror-like, shone through the trees and as that hot, airless afternoon lengthened, I was sorely tempted to go for a swim. And I know if we'd had so much as a leaky rowboat, I would have suggested starting out for Turkey. However, Englhardt pointed out that not only might I be spotted on the beach if I went swimming, but since we were already suffering from thirst—we'd finished our water that morning—the salt water would only make it worse.

I agreed with him. But I didn't agree with him when he suggested later that instead of continuing westward to the mountains we return to Kerch.

"Are you crazy?" I asked irritably. "Every cop and possibly even the Red Army will be concentrated in that area!"

"I don't think so," he replied pensively. "Tonight will be the fifth night since I escaped. In other words, they've had four days in which to search the port. It is my opinion that by now they will have decided I'm not there and spread out. So if we go down to Feodosiya or one of the other ports to look for a ship, we will stand more chance of running into them."

"Could be that you're right." Reluctantly, I admitted the soundness of his argument. "But I don't fancy returning to Kerch." I recalled those two flat-eyed plainclothesmen. If they heard I was back in the port it would be pushing my luck too far, I decided, to expect them to believe I was still the innocent tourist.

"Besides," he went on, "we already know a man with a boat. And it seems much simpler to me to go back and convince him that he should take us, rather than begin to look for another man in another port."

"Which makes sense. The only snag is that I was stupid enough not to get his name and not even the name of the boat. In fact, I don't even know where he lives."

"We can contact him through the woman you told me about. The woman who owns the shop."

Slowly, I shook my head. "I don't trust any of them. Those characters aren't stupid and they'll have heard of the escape and realize now the connection between the food parcel and my request for a boat."

"We can afford to be generous—"

"In any other country I'd say yes, that if we paid enough we'd get a boat." I shrugged. "But I'm beginning to believe that in Russia, smuggling nationals across frontiers is not a purchasable occupation, if you know what I mean."

"I have an idea I might succeed."

His voice was full of confidence, but I was still apprehensive. I remembered that teen-ager sitting on the bed beside me, watching the mickey-finn she had poured me take effect. And when they learned that Englhardt was the fugitive from the prison camp, they'd accept all the money we offered—and then hedge their bet by selling us to the police.

"Well," I said finally, "you're a Russian and should know more about these people than I do. And if you think you can make a deal—" I glanced up at the purple sunset "—let's get going. We've got a long ride ahead of us. Besides, if I sit here any longer my nerves are going to start twanging."

For a long moment he stared at me. "I've a better idea," he said. "As you have pointed out, you're not a Russian. You don't speak the language, and therefore you'll be no help in Kerch. In fact—" he smiled "—you'll only be a hindrance since it's twice as difficult for two people to keep out of sight as one. You stay here. When I have arranged for the boat, we'll come and pick you up from the cove."

"Sure," I said, returning his smile with a grin. "That's a swell idea. We should have thought of it sooner. The only thing is, you've got it slightly twisted. You stay here and I'll go get the boat. I know them, and as for speaking Russian, I told you the Rat speaks English."

"No," he protested, "you've already done your share—"

"Oh, nuts!" I muttered, standing up. "You have no intention of staying and neither have I, so let's get on our way. Besides, I'm looking forward to a bottle of hennahaired Tanya's vodka, unspiked."

The dogs were beginning to forage and the cocks to crow when we reached the outskirts of Kerch. We hid the bicycles in a patch of underbrush and, rubbing a certain part of my anatomy which had become extremely sensitive, I sincerely hoped I'd never see them again. Keeping to the side streets and alleyways, we made our way down to the port as fast as we could but it was almost daylight when we reached the shop. And I discovered I was as nervous as I was that last night I'd been in the city. I cursed Englhardt for not waiting on the coast. The half-light made his hulking shoulders seem to stretch from wall to wall in the narrow streets. Any fool, I thought, would recognize him as the giant who had escaped from the prison camp. I cursed myself for letting him talk me into retracing our steps. It was madness to come back here where we were both so well known.

I knocked impatiently on the door, but for a long time there was no response from within. Three or four shadowy figures wandered by, their eyes on us, and my nervousness increased.

Englhardt's cool nonchalance as he leaned up against the building, hands in pockets, didn't help matters any.

Finally a light shone and Tanya, clutching a negligee about her sagging body, appeared. She stared through the glass panel, recognized me, and shook her head. I wrapped my handkerchief around my fist, and began to bang on the glass. I had every intention of breaking it, which she must have realized. Eventually she waved an admonishing hand and unlocked the door. At that moment, Englhardt moved into view, and she tried to shut it again. But he was too quick for her. He pushed the door open, stepped inside and with a wide-mouthed grin bade her good morning.

"You can't stay here!" she muttered in German and her voice was full of fear.

"We don't intend to," Englhardt said easily. "But let us go inside where it is more private."

She stared at him, her eyes partly closed, and I could almost see her alert brain summing him up. Finally with a resigned shrug, she closed the door, locked it and led us down the passage to the gold room. She snapped on a lamp.

"What do you want?" Her question was directed at Englhardt. In fact, after that first moment at the door, she hadn't so much as glanced at me.

He gave her his most charming smile. "First a drink. The best wine you have and I hope you will join us." He sat down on the couch and stretched out his legs. "These roads are dusty."

She stood there, her bare feet wide apart, glaring down at him and I couldn't help but admire his ease and poise. He might have been asking the waiter at Maxime's to bring a bottle of champagne.

"It's too late," she protested. "Why do you come here?"

"I told you. We're thirsty."

She threw a quick glance over her shoulder and when she discovered me blocking the doorway, she must have decided the quickest way to get rid of us was to humor us.

"All right," she said coldly, "and then you'll have to go. I don't want the police here."

"Police?" Englhardts eyebrows lifted. "Why should they come unless you send for them?"

"You take me for a fool?" Her lip curled. "I know who you are."

"In that case, introductions aren't necessary."

She waddled over to the cabinet and got out a long-necked bottle of the local white wine and two glasses. While she was drawing the cork, I moved into the room, closed the door behind me and quietly twisted the key.

"And you?" Englhardt said when she'd filled both glasses.

"I don't like the stuff." But when she noticed me pick up my drink and sniff it, she gave me the full benefit of contemptuous eyes. "Don't worry, it's all right," she taunted. "All I wish is for you to get out of here—on your own feet."

I grinned at her and gulped down the warm, overly sweet wine, and it tasted like nectar. I refilled my glass and sat down on a chair near the door.

"Where's your sailor friend?" Englhardt asked casually. "We waited two nights on the beach for him."

"You think he's crazy?" Her black eyes were suddenly wary as they flicked over Englhardt. "He agreed to take this American— not an escaped convict."

Englhardt slowly nodded and sipped his wine. "I understand. But my friend here was afraid he couldn't trust him if he told him the truth. How can we get in touch with him?"

"You're wasting your time. They're searching the whole country for you and he wouldn't take you now for a million roubles."

"Oh, come, come," Englhardt laughed. "I'm not that important."

"No. Not you." She shrugged and I noticed with sardonic amusement the affect of Englhardt's personality. Her hostile expression gradually faded and I wasn't surprised when she got out a bottle of vodka and poured herself a glassful.

"What do you mean, I'm not?"

"It's this foreigner here—" she indicated me with a toss of her head "—who's caused all the excitement."

"You mean they know he helped me escape?"

"What did you expect? He'd been loitering around the port for a week, buying bicycles, stocking up with food and then disappearing the same night you escape." I felt like something hanging on the wall the way she discussed me without so much as a glance in my direction. "How is it," she went on, "they didn't find you on the coast?"

"Obviously because they didn't search carefully enough. What else do you know?"

She poured herself another thimble of vodka and Englhardt handed me the wine bottle.

"They came here asking what he'd been doing in my place," she said.

"And you told them he'd been looking for a ship."

"You think I'm a fool? If I'd told them that, they'd have run me in for not reporting it sooner. I said he was fooling around with my daughter."

Englhardt grinned at me. "So that's what you've been doing!"

I smiled weakly, but I was in no mood to match his banter. The news that they were searching for me and that they were more interested in finding me than Englhardt, turned my blood to ice water. I had always realized that if Englhardt was recaptured and I was found with him, I'd certainly be suspected of helping him. But I was not prepared for this sudden recasting which had apparently given me the principal role in this drama. And I thought I'd been so cunning in covering up my tracks!

"Let's get on with it," I said with nervous impatience. "How can we get hold of this sailor?"

"I keep telling you it's no use," she persisted. "It's too dangerous."

"Let him decide that," I muttered.

"No hurry," Englhardt put in. "He's probably still asleep anyway. May I try the vodka?"

She pushed the bottle closer to him and he filled her glass as well as his own. He asked her if they were still searching the port and she said no, that after the first morning, the police knew we had fled to the country. And if they hadn't been sure to begin with, she pointed out, the nails we'd scattered soon proved it. "That's probably why they didn't catch you the first night," she said with a laugh. "They were too busy repairing their tires."

"Then we can relax," Englhardt said, clinking his glass against hers. "Tell me about your friend, the sailor. What kind of a boat has he got?"

"A fishing boat."

"He a fisherman?"

She smiled. "Most of the time."

His wink was broad. "I understand. We thought his engine had broken down."

"Sasha's engine can't afford to break down. I told you—he wasn't interested when he heard who he was supposed to take."

"Where does he keep the boat?"

"Down at the fish wharf."

"Is it a big boat? I mean, are there several sailors he'd have to cut in on the deal?"

"No, it's not so big. He works it with one other man."

"But fast?"

"Fast enough," she said knowingly. "But you're wasting your time even thinking about it."

Englhardt refilled the glasses. "Maybe he has a friend who is not so timid."

"Maybe." She leaned back in the chair and crossed her legs and I noticed Englhardt raise an eyebrow as he inspected a large expanse of bare thigh. "You can ask him," she went on.

"That's what I'd like to do. How be you send for him?"

"I don't want you hanging around here."

"But we don't know where to find him."

"Go down to the port. He lives on his boat. Just ask anyone for the *Natasha*."

He laughed easily. "By now it's daylight. How far do you think we'd get without being picked up?"

"That's your lookout," she said petulantly, picking up her glass. "And now you'd better finish up and get out of here before I have to open the shop."

"You know, we have quite a lot of money to spend."

"Huh!" she snorted. "And what good will money do me in Siberia?"

He hunched forward on the couch. "No one is going to Siberia. The police think we're on the other side of the peninsula. You've just said so yourself. So stop worrying about it. Send your daughter down to the dock with a message for Sasha to come and see you. We'll talk to him and if he still won't take us or find someone who will, we'll go and leave you alone."

"Olga's still asleep." But I knew from the tone of her voice that she was weakening.

The shop didn't open that morning. By the time Englhardt and the woman had finished the bottle of vodka, they were sitting on the couch together. From Tanya's periodic gurgles of coarse laughter, I presumed he was running through his repertoire of Rabelaisian stories. I had moved into an armchair and despite my taut nerves, it wasn't long before the combination of wine and no sleep took effect.

A persistent knocking on the door awakened me and I opened my eyes in time to see Tanya weave across the room and unlock it. Olga appeared and immediately I snapped alert. A quick glance at Englhardt told me he was listening carefully to what the two women were saying. Even so, I got up and walked over to the door and held out my hand.

I looked over her shoulder as we shook hands. The hallway was empty. She smiled and walked into the room. Tanya got another bottle out of the cabinet and I closed the door and stole a quick glance at my watch. It was twelve-thirty and I suddenly realized I was starving.

Englhardt and the girl spoke together for a few minutes while Tanya refilled the glasses. I needed another drink like I needed a hole in the head, but I was afraid to refuse. Tanya's black eyes were glazed and she'd long since given up trying to restrain the negligee. Englhardt was pale, but his eyes were clear. I moved over beside him and asked him quietly in English how he was getting along.

"We're safe enough for the moment," he said. "I'm going to ask the girl to get the boatman."

"You think it's wise? She won't go somewhere else?" I didn't want to mention the word police.

"Have to take that chance."

"Well, we're stuck here now. It's noon."

"Yes," he muttered disconsolately, "my stomach tells me." He turned and spoke to Tanya in Russian. She looked at me, laughed, and said something to her daughter. A moment later Olga went out.

"I said you couldn't hold your liquor," Englhardt explained to me, "and that she'd better give you something to eat."

Olga brought in several dishes of smoked fish, cold meat and cold vegetables and spread them out on the table. Tanya waved an expansive hand and invited me to help myself. I started but it wasn't long before the others joined me.

When we had finished everything in sight, Olga disappeared and Englhardt told me to keep my fingers crossed. I moved back to the armchair and spent the next couple of hours suffering from nervous indigestion. And with Bacchanalian abandon, my two companions fell asleep on the couch.

The girl returned at four-thirty with the news that Sasha, the fisherman, was busy helping another man fix his engine, and that he would come to the shop as soon as they were finished. Olga seemed very natural and unconcerned and I relaxed and told Englhardt with a grin that he'd been right in suggesting that we return to Kerch. For I was sure that Sasha would not be able to refuse once Englhardt went to work on him. I wished I had more money on me. But it didn't worry me; I felt that even if we had to pay more, Englhardt would arrange it somehow.

Tanya finally decided that it was time she got dressed. Leaving Olga to entertain us, she went upstairs. She returned wearing the flowered-silk number and about seven ounces of perfume. Englhardt stood up and bowed and said something that drew forth a girlish giggle.

One hour later there was a solid knock on the door. But before anyone could get up and open it, two men pushed into the room. My jaw dropped and automatically I started to my feet.

They were the two flat-eyed plainclothesmen. And behind them, a smirk twisting his ugly features, was Sasha the Rat.

"Good evening, Mr. Sherman," the first policeman said, a sardonic smile on his lips. "And I presume this is your friend, Nicholas Englhardt."

"I don't think I know these gentlemen." Englhardt's voice was smooth.

"Police—" I stuttered.

"So." And without a flicker of an eyelash, he stared up at the two men. "We've been expecting you," he said in English. "I was afraid this *verdampt* woman had sent for you."

"Come on, let's go," the policeman said brusquely.

Englhardt picked up his glass and slowly stood up. "May I?" he asked with an engaging smile. "Probably the last drink I shall have for some years."

And then with a quick flick of his wrist he dashed the vodka into the policeman's face. The man let out a yell and clutched at his eyes and I finally snapped out of it and made a lunge for the second man as he was drawing a gun from a shoulder holster. I got my hands on his wrist and after struggling for a few moments the gun went off between us. With a surge of panic-driven strength, I broke the gun out of his grip before he could fire again and it clattered to the floor. He brought his knee up and I felt scarlet pain. I hit him in the face but it was like hitting a solid rock. He caught me on the side of the head and I went over a chair and landed on my shoulders in a corner. He came at me with both feet but I twisted away and took his kick on the shoulder. I grabbed his leg and pulled him down and we rolled about the floor smashing everything in our way. He got his hands on my throat and I was beginning to gasp for breath when I heard a dull thud close to my ear and he stiffened out in my arms.

Slowly and painfully I crawled to my knees, panting for breath. Englhardt was standing over me, an empty bottle in his hand.

"You all right?" he asked anxiously.

"I dunno," I mumbled. "That bastard doesn't know the rules."

I crawled into a chair and looked around. The room was a shambles. The first policeman was stretched out on the floor, his face a bloody pulp. Sasha was lying on his face, and from the way his body was twisted, I had the feeling he was dead. Olga was huddled behind what was left of the phonograph, and Tanya was sitting on the couch, pouring a drink and quietly laughing to herself.

"That must have been quite a fight I missed," I said, rubbing my sore face. "What happened?"

Englhardt carefully set a table back on its legs and put the bottle down. "The vodka blinded the first man which made it easy for me to incapacitate him," he explained. "Our former friend, Sasha, got in the way of that stray bullet and you very ably kept the second man occupied until I could help you."

"It's too bad that bitch sitting there laughing didn't stop the bullet," I muttered. "When did she send for the police? When she was dressing?"

"Come, come, my friend," he said, straightening his clothes. "You are maligning our hostess. I'm sure she doesn't like informers any more than we do."

"But you told the police it was her—"

"A red herring. After all, she has to live here. I have a feeling it was the sailor. Obviously he arrived earlier, overheard our voices from the hallway and went and got the police. We've been very careless."

"Which makes everything just dandy! Now what do we do?"

"First, get some rope." He spoke to Tanya and she went out and brought back several lengths of stout cord. Expertly, he bound the wrists and legs of the two unconscious men. Then with strips torn from a pillow, he gagged them.

"What time is it?" he asked.

I glanced at my watch but the face had been smashed in. "Must be about six-thirty or seven," I said.

"See how dark it is outside. The sooner we can leave the better."

I went out to the shop. The sun had set, but the after-glow was still strong. It would be another half hour before we could safely venture out into the streets. And to go where, I asked myself with complete dejection. The only man we knew with a boat was lying dead in there and we had two policemen on our hands. True, we could keep them prisoner, but how long before they would be missed? One hour? Two hours? About time enough for us to retrieve the bicycles if they hadn't already been discovered. And the questionable security of the mountains was over a night's ride away...

As for trying to hide in Kerch, once those cops were freed, they'd burn down the port if necessary to find us. I returned to the gold room dragging my spirits behind me.

"Not quite dark," I said disconsolately, "but what difference it makes I wouldn't know."

Englhardt looked at me, laughed, and said, "What you need is a drink."

"That's for sure. I also need to know how we're going to get out of this bloody town—out of this bloody country."

"The same way you had originally planned."

"Sure." I nodded towards the dead man. "And there's our skipper. By the time we find another boat, every cop in Crimea will be watching the waterfront."

"Another boat?" he said brightly. "What's wrong with Sasha's *Natasha?*"

Slowly I shook my head. But there was no question about it; his complete confidence was lifting me out of my depression. "And what do we do with these police? Sooner or later they'll be missed."

"Exactly. So the sooner we start the better." He turned to Tanya. "I'm afraid there is no way we can pay you now for this damage. If we gave you foreign money they would arrest you when you tried to exchange it."

"Forget it." Her smoldering black eyes were on his as she waved a magnanimous hand. "If I didn't have that girl to look after I would go with you."

He bowed gallantly. "It would give me great pleasure. But I'm afraid that under the circumstances your journey would be dangerous."

She laughed. "Almost as dangerous as being left here with these two." She spurned the nearest policeman with her toe.

"We will tie you both up and lock you in one of the rooms upstairs," he explained. "It will be better than leaving you with them here. They might ask too many questions before you are all released. When you are freed, you tell them it was you who sent Sasha to get them. They will have no reason for not believing you."

She shrugged and stood up. "I suppose it would be smarter." And then with a curt nod to her daughter, she went out. I started to say thanks and goodbye, but she walked past me without so much as a glance. It was obvious that the only man in her house was Nicholas Englhardt. He picked up what was left of the cord and followed her.

"And now," he said when he returned a few minutes later, "let us go and find the *Natasha*."

CHAPTER FOURTEEN

THE FISH DOCK was almost deserted. Most of the boats had departed for the night's work and the few remaining were dark, silent hulls, their crews dispersed ashore. Englhardt paused beside a solitary, ancient mariner sitting on a bollard and spoke to him for several moments. The man finally shuffled to his feet and led us at a slow gait along the outer quay. He stopped before three boats moored together, bow on the quay, and indicated the middle one. I tried to make out the name but it was too dark. Englhardt thanked our guide and a minute or so later, he turned and disappeared into the murk.

I pulled on the mooring rope until the bow was close enough to the dock for us to jump on board. "Check the name," I whispered, "and I'll see if there is anyone around."

Quietly I ran aft and looked into the small wheelhouse. It was empty and no light showed from the narrow companionway leading below.

"It's the *Natasha*, all right," Englhardt said, joining me. "The name is painted on the bow. Do you know anything about boats?"

"Not much. And you?"

"Nothing. They make me seasick."

"Good God! Had we better wait and shanghai the sailor?"

He turned and stared back at the port. "What do you think?" he asked quietly. "You're the captain."

"I think we're a couple of damned fools for not returning to the mountains," I muttered, my temper thoroughly shortened by nervousness. "Anyway, I'll see what kind of an engine this tub's got."

The *Natasha* was about forty feet long with an enormous beam and flush decks. She was solidly if roughly built of heavy timbers and since there was no trawling gear on board I presumed Sacha had used either nets or long lines for fishing. Between the fish hatch and the wheelhouse was an iron skylight and I could make out the black mass of an engine when I peered down. The entrance to the engine room, I discovered, was through the companionway in the wheelhouse.

It required half a box of matches to learn that the engine was a heavy diesel similar to a Swedish Bolinder, that it was started by compressed air and that the air bottle was three quarters full. The fuel tanks were almost full and the oil level in the sump was normal. I traced the throttle and gear levers to the wheelhouse and after locating the starting handle, returned to the deck.

"I think I can start the engine," I said. "But if this tub does more than eight knots I'll buy her."

"Careful!" Englhardt warned and we ducked behind the wheelhouse. Two men strolled along the quay, paused in front of the next boat, and for a long dreadful moment I thought they were going aboard. Finally, they moved on.

"If we're going," I said hurriedly, "let's get the hell on our way. The next thing we know those cops will come running along that quay." I had a last, quick look around. It was quiet, deathly quiet, and I knew the bark of that heavy engine starting up would be heard all along the waterfront.

"When you hear the engine going," I said, "let go the bow line and pull the boat out by the rope at the stern. It's probably fastened to an anchor but be careful you don't get the rope tangled in the propellor."

"Which way do we go?"

"See those red and green lights? They mark the entrance to the harbor. We go between them and then it's up to God to navigate us down to the sea. But I'll come up as soon as I get the engine started." The pale moonlight shone on his big teeth as he grinned at me, and I went below with the thought that he'd grin at his own funeral.

I flipped the light switch but there was no response. Either the batteries were dead or there weren't any. I found a stub of a candle in one of the tool drawers, lit it and stuck it on the bench. I turned on the fuel, primed the pump and with my heart pounding somewhere up in my throat, pulled the starting handle. With a loud hiss of air, the engine turned over but didn't fire. I closed the air valve and glanced at the pressure. It was down to half and I knew that if the engine didn't catch before that bottle was empty we would have to swim for it.

I primed the fuel pump again and pulled the starting handle. The engine fired once and died. I closed the valve again. The pressure was down to a quarter. Carefully, I checked the engine again to see if there were any starting gadgets I'd missed. Everything appeared to be in order.

I wiped the sweat out of my eyes and once more primed the pump. And then with a silent prayer I gave her the rest of the bottle. She fired—missed—fired—missed—and then with a deafening, boat-shaking roar, caught. I eased back the throttle and, ten years older, climbed the ladder to the deck.

The bowline was already gone and Englhardt was pulling us away from the dock by the stern line. I gave him a hand and was sure that the deep, rhythmic *bomb bomb bomb* of the engine's exhaust could be heard in Moscow. When we were well out in the harbor I told Englhardt to forget about the anchor and slowly feed the rope back out when we moved ahead. I jumped into the wheelhouse, shoved the gear handle forward and opened the throttle. The little ship gradually lost sternway, paused, then started slowly forward. I banged the throttle wide open and spun the wheel to the left as far as it would go. We came around in a wide turn and I straightened her out and headed for a point equidistant between the red and green entrance lights.

Englhardt came and stood by the wheelhouse door. "All clear, captain!" he called out cheerfully.

"Any sign of excitement back on the dock?"

"Not yet."

"There will be!" I muttered.

The marking lights were opening up now and the *Natasha* was picking up speed.

"What's that smell?" Englhardt said, shoving his head into the wheelhouse.

"God Almighty!" I cursed, suddenly catching the acrid smell of burning oil. "Take the wheel!" I closed the throttle and started down the ladder.

"What do I do?" Englhardt said, fumbling at the wheel.

"Go between those lights!" I shouted. "Steer it like a car!"

The manifold glowed dull red in the smoke-filled engine room and I could hear the paint cracking. After a frantic search and a badly scorched hand I found the sea-cock leading to the water pump and opened it. Gradually the engine began to cool off. My knees trembling, I climbed back to the deck.

"Forgot to turn on the water," I panted, gulping down the sweet night air. "And I thought I knew about engines!"

We were passing between the lights now and a group of shadowy figures standing on the end of one of the quays stared down at us. It was impossible in the darkness to see whether they were wearing uniforms or not. Englhardt leaned out and waved at them.

"Friends of yours?" I asked sarcastically.

"Might as well let them think so. Besides, it's probably the last time I'll ever see my native country."

"I sincerely hope so," I said quietly.

We lurched out into the strait and corkscrewed south. Englhardt tended to overcorrect everytime the bow fell off, but since I wasn't too sure I could do any better, I left him at the wheel and kept one eye on the engine, the other on the murky shore. He was loving every minute of it, and when I asked him if he was feeling seasick yet, he roared with laughter and said no, that I hadn't given him time to even think of it. I was trying to rig up the candle so he could see the compass needle when I discovered a paraffin lamp inside the binnacle.

So far as I could remember from the map Sasha had given me and which I'd stupidly left behind in the pack, it was fifteen or twenty miles to the open sea. I had no idea of the actual speed we were making. The water was oily calm and we appeared to be travelling at a terrific rate. But I did know that at night a ship's speed was very deceiving and I figured that it would take us an hour and a half to two hours to reach the Black Sea.

An hour must have passed and the only sign of activity was the lights of a ship several miles off to our right and heading in the opposite direction. I pointed them out to Englhardt and suggested that since that skipper obviously knew the course, we must be away off. He said that it was quite possible as the strait opened up like a lake in the center, narrowing again at the entrance to the sea. I asked him why the hell he hadn't told me that before, and he said that he presumed, since I'd been in Kerch for a week, I'd known it. I told him to head more to the southwest.

I went down and checked the engine again. The temperature was normal and the air pressure up so I shut off the compressor. I was trying to discover what was wrong with the generator when I heard Englhardt calling me.

"Here they come!" he said, and for the first time that night, there was a note of excitement in his voice.

I looked across to the right and saw the long finger of a searchlight sweeping back and forth across the surface of the water. The boat it was on was going twice our speed.

"Head her back to the left!" I cried. "Maybe they'll miss us if we're so far over!"

"What about that engine? Won't they hear it?"

"I don't know, but we'll shut it off anyway."

By the time I got back to the deck the patrol boat was opposite us and about three or four miles away. And so far as I could judge, they hadn't changed course.

"Well, they gave us a good start," Englhardt said, nonchalantly leaning out of the window.

"But not good enough," I said bitterly. "All they have to do now is sit in the entrance and we'll never get out."

We both glanced up as a raft of thin cloud slid across the moon. "If it would only rain," he said.

"If we'd lived right; it would. Or there'd be a fog."

Nervously I lit a cigarette, my eyes following that probing searchlight. Now that ours was silent, I could hear the distant roar of powerful, fast-revving engines. But the patrol boat didn't alter course and gradually the searchlight faded into the night.

"No use sitting here like a tired duck," I said finally. "When they discover they've missed us they'll be back."

"Which direction will we go?"

"Our only hope is to keep in as close to shore as possible. After the moon sets we just might be able to dodge out to sea."

"Can you make that engine more quiet?"

"Sure," I said drily, "I can shut it off and paddle."

His laugh boomed out. "I told you I didn't know anything about boats!"

"You'll learn, my friend, before this night is over," I said, going below.

The shore line came out of the murk and we turned south and followed it. And the hair of an experienced sailor would have turned gray had he attempted to follow our course as we dodged around rocky headlands and cut across beaches. But with the luck of the completely ignorant, we touched no rocks or shoals. Englhardt continued to handle the helm and I stood in the bow directing him.

The moon was riding low when we picked up the flashing light marking the entrance to the channel. It was away off to the west and I presumed it was on the western shore. There was no sign of the patrol boat and I wondered if she was sitting out there, her engines and lights off, waiting for us.

I walked back to the wheelhouse. Englhardt was lounging out the window, one big hand on the wheel, humming to himself.

"You know," he said, "I'm going to buy a yacht. I've decided I like this life."

"You're absolutely incorrigible," I said, shaking my head. "We're about one jump ahead of a machine gun and all you can think of is buying a yacht."

"I don't like thinking of machine guns."

I took a rough bearing of the light from the lighthouse and as far as I could make out by the shifting compass, we were due east of it.

"For all I know," I said, "we might have already reached the sea. That light appears to be abreast of us."

"In that case, I congratulate you, captain!"

"Huh! You can congratulate me when you feel Turkish soil under your feet. They'll capture us even if they find us within sight of the other shore."

The moon had set when we saw the patrol boat again. She came charging up from the south, her searchlight still sweeping. I told Englhardt to head straight in towards the shore, jumped down and turned off the engine.

And then our luck ran out. We were both looking astern, our eyes glued to the approaching patrol boat, when I felt the *Natasha* shudder and come to an abrupt halt as she slid up on something solid. I ran forward and looked over the bow. A score or more yards ahead was the grayish line of a beach.

Slowly, my spirits as damp as the water surrounding us, I walked back and sat down on the bulwark. "That does it," I said, fumbling for a cigarette. "If they don't find us now, they certainly will when the sun comes up."

"You mean, we're stuck here?"

"That, my friend, is known as an understatement." I glanced up at him. "You still interested in yachts?"

"Why don't we push her off?"

"Push this tub? She must weigh twenty tons!"

"Oh ..." He put his hand on my shoulder. "I'm sorry," he said quietly, "it seems that I only bring you—"

"Hell! It's not your fault any more than mine. Less. I've been completely stupid all the way down the line. In view of what we don't know about boats, I was stupid to even consider stealing one. As for leaving that map behind ...!" He drifted off forward and I sat there staring at the glowing end of the cigarette, wondering how old I'd be when they let us out of the mines.

Sometime later I heard a splash. Englhardt had stripped and was standing up to his chest in the water.

"You going ashore?" I called out.

"Not yet. But I think we can move this boat."

I felt the *Natasha* rock as he leaned against it with his power-ful shoulder. "Well," I said without much enthusiasm, "we can but try." I took off my clothes.

The water was warm, soupy and the bottom sandy. Which should mean, I told myself with reviving spirits, that we hadn't knocked a hole in her. But when the two of us pushed the bow it was like trying to push Gibraltar. The heavy hull would rock back and forth but she wouldn't budge an inch backward.

"I've got an idea!" I said suddenly, climbing back on board. "Come and help me."

Starting at the bow, we tossed every detachable object over-board. We pulled out the anchor chain by hand, unfastened it and let it go with the anchor. We took apart as much of the winch as would come apart and dropped it over the side. Moving aft, we stripped off hatch covers, fish boxes—everything that wasn't bolted to the deck.

"Let's try her," I said, when we'd reached the stern. I slipped back into the water. It seemed much deeper. "She's afloat!" I yelled. "Stay on board!"

I pushed her out until I was swimming, caught hold of the side and pulled myself on board. "Let's get out of here before we drift ashore again. You see that patrol boat?"

"No. I'd forgotten about her."

And in the excitement, so had I. We searched the night but there was no sign of her. She may have returned to Kerch—or she might be quietly sitting out there waiting for us to start our engine. But we had to do. something or we would drift back on the beach.

I started the engine and slowly backed away.

When we had room to turn, I swung her around and headed due south and opened the throttle wide. "And now, Mr. Mate," I said, "I suggest we stop fooling around the shore and head for Turkey as fast as we can. We've only got three or four hours of darkness left and if we're still near the coast come daylight even the gendarmes will spot us."

"Aye aye, captain," he said with a grin and took the wheel while I got dressed.

The dawn was soft, pearl-gray and beautiful and there wasn't a breeze to ruffle the surface of the sea. I would have preferred a thick fog or at least a howling rain storm. The land had dropped out of sight astern and there was no other ship in sight. Neither of us had a watch but it seemed to me we must have put fifty miles between us and the Crimea. I suggested to Englhardt that he get some sleep, and that I'd call him in a couple of hours. One minute later he was curled up in a corner of the wheelhouse softly snoring. I'd have given a lot for that man's steel nerves.

The sun was almost directly overhead when we heard the sound of a light airplane. I banged the throttle closed, shoved the gear into neutral and ran out to the stern.

"Give me a hand!" I shouted to Englhardt, and tossed the end of a heavy rope over the side. I played it out as the ship gradually slowed up. "Get that other rope into the water. Quick!"

He tossed several coils of the rope overboard. Slowly they sank and straightened out. The plane was in sight now, heading towards us from the west in a shallow dive.

"They're searching for us!" I said. "Make like we're fishing!"

"What? With these ropes?" He threw me a startled look.

"They won't know there's not a net on the end."

The plane, with Russian military markings, flew directly overhead, turned and circled a hundred feet off the water. It was an open two-seater monoplane and we could plainly see the goggled faces staring across at us. We waved, but they didn't wave back. It circled closer and the man in the rear cockpit gestured towards the north.

"He's telling us to return," I said.

Englhardt's laugh boomed out. "He'll have to come on board and make us!"

I waved again and gestured towards the ropes in the water.

And then I caught sight of a black object resting on the edge of the cockpit. "Look out!" I shouted. "I think he's got a gun!" I heard the crack of a shot over the engine noise. "Into the fish hatch!"

Letting the rope go, I ran forward and jumped into the open hatch. Englhardt's heavy body landed beside me. I glanced over the combing. The plane was practically standing on its wing now, the circles were so tight. I heard another shot and ducked.

Englhardt was squatting under the deck checking the magazine of a revolver. "Where in the hell did you get that?" I demanded.

He smiled. "Off the floor in Tanya's house. But I'm afraid there are only five bullets left."

"Never mind! Just wave it at them. That should be enough to make them keep their distance."

"I hope so. I wouldn't like to kill anyone."

He stood up, rested his elbow on the hatch combing and took a long time aiming. Finally he pulled the trigger. Almost immediately, the plane flipped over and started to climb away.

"Good God, you've hit it! Wonderful!" I cried.

"I hardly think so," he said drily, "since I aimed well behind it."

The plane, still climbing, began to circle again. But it kept well out of range. And then I saw the glint of sunlight on wire as they began to unreel a trailing antenna.

"There goes their aerial," I said. "They're going to call up the reserves."

"In that case, hadn't we better start again?" Englhardt said, putting away the gun. "They certainly know who we are."

Once more we headed south, the little ship shaking at the seams with the vibration of the racing engine. The plane continued to circle us, high up, for fifteen or twenty minutes, then broke away and disappeared into the north.

"If they've sent for the fighters," I muttered, "you'd better keep two of those bullets for us."

But the minutes dragged past and no other planes appeared. "It would seem," Englhardt said finally, "that they have called for the patrol boat. They obviously wish to take us alive. Can it catch us before nightfall?"

"I don't know. Figure it out. If that patrol boat does twice our speed, she's going to take half the time we took to get out here. What time do you think it is now?"

For several moments he studied the sun. "I'd say about one o'clock."

"Well, we left the shore around three in the morning. Ten hours cruising. Therefore if it takes them five hours, they'll be up to us by six this evening—with still a couple of hours of daylight left in which to find us."

"That is," he said cheerfully, "if we stand still."

"You're almost as good a mathematician as you are a sailor," I said, suddenly grinning at him. "Of course I forgot we'll be moving ahead. So that means they won't be up to us until it's dark!" I pounded him on the back. "Englhardt, I think we're going to make it!" I turned more to the southwest. "But just to make sure, let's get off the course that plane will have reported we're following." And for the first time in twenty-four hours I felt very hungry.

CHAPTER FIFTEEN

IT MUST HAVE been seven-thirty or eight o'clock that evening when we noticed the hull of a steamer approaching us from the east. And unless we altered course, we would pass very close to her.

"If she's a Russian," I told Englhardt, "she may have been warned to be on the lookout for us. I think we'd better swing around."

"Wait." He was silent for a long time as he studied the oncoming ship. "I wish we had a pair of binoculars," he said, finally.

"Well, let's not take any chances." I turned the *Natasha* to the west.

"No, keep going south." He glanced up at the sky. "It will be dark soon and if she is a Russian, we can lose her. And if she's not, I have an idea."

I swung back on the original course. "Make up your mind," I said, watching the ship. "She'll be crossing our bow in five minutes or so."

"I've been thinking that when we land on the Turkish coast, you will be all right. You're an American and have your passport," he said slowly, pensively. "As for me, I have nothing, not even that false Belgian *carte d'identité.* It is in Brussels. And if the Turkish police pick us up—"

"The same thought had been going through my mind," I admitted. "But why can't you say you're a refugee seeking political asylum?"

"I could, but I'm afraid that when the Russians explain that I'm an escaped convict and not a political refugee, the Turks might hand me over. However, whatever they decide, they'll take weeks to make up their mind."

"I see your point. And in the meantime you're warming a stone bench in some Turkish jail."

"Possibly. If not a jail, certainly a refugee camp."

"But I can explain—"

"What?" He laughed. "That we weren't working together to the detriment of the USSR Ministry of Trade?"

"Well ..."

"No, my friend. You still have a commercial life ahead of you. You must as of now forget you ever knew me. I only hope that already I haven't damaged your reputation."

"Don't worry. No one who matters knows anything about our relationship. But what's all this got to do with that ship that's coming up?"

"This: if she's not a Russian, she's probably a Greek or Italian tanker out of Batum. In that case I suggest we get them to pick us up. Thus we will definitely avoid recapture by the patrol boat and also it will give me more time to consider my next move."

"Sounds like a good idea," I said. "But if they see us steaming along under our own power, why should they pick us up?"

"I hadn't thought of that. Let us shut off the engine and make distress signals. We can say the engine is broken."

Doubtfully, I shook my head. "And if she's Russian?"

"We start up and run for it."

"I hope you know what you're doing," I said, going below. "Try to make out her flag as soon as you can."

The *Natasha* wallowed quietly in the trough of the sea, almost in the track of the approaching ship. Both of us stood at the rail straining our eyes to see what flag if any she was flying, but from that angle it was impossible to even see her stern.

"She's turning to avoid us," I said. "Probably thinks we have nets out."

"S—A—N—" Englhardt spelled out slowly, reading the name off the bow. To my eyes it was still a blur. *"San Giovanni!"* he cried a moment later. "Italian!" He stripped off his shirt and began to wave it.

I could make out the name now and also that she was a small, battered tanker with her rust patches glowing in the afterlight of the sun. A man appeared on the wing of the bridge and trained his glasses on us. He called to someone inside the wheelhouse and another man joined him and for several moments they stood there staring at us. The tanker continued on her way, passing about a quarter of a mile astern of the *Natasha*.

"Damn it! She's going right on!" I said, grimly, taking off my shirt and frantically waving it. "Supposing we really were in distress?"

Several sailors lined the rails watching us. Two or three of them waved.

"They think we're just saying hello," Englhardt chuckled. "What do you do when you're in trouble at sea?"

"God! I don't know!" I gestured towards the propellor and waved my hands sideways. At last one of the men on the bridge returned to the wheelhouse.

"She's turning!" Englhardt cried. "What shall we say is wrong with the engine?"

"Ah—bearing. Tell them we've burned out a bearing."

We heard the engine room bell clang, and the tanker gradually lost way, as she swung in towards us. More sailors now crowded along the rail.

The man on the wing of the bridge put away his binoculars and stared down at us. He needed a shave and the unbuttoned white tunic he was wearing was very dirty.

Cupping his hands, Englhardt called out in Italian, asking him if it was an Italian ship. It was, the man said, and what was

our trouble? Englhardt explained that we'd burned out a bearing.
The Italian shrugged and said that he couldn't tow us, that he was
going direct to the Bosporus and it would take too long.

"We don't want a tow," Englhardt explained. "We want to
come on board."

"And what will you do with your ship?"

"Let her sink. She will anyway now that the pump's not
working."

I stole a glance at Englhardt. For a man who knew nothing
about boats, he was doing all right.

"Where are you from?"

"Careful," I whispered, "he may be an Italian Communist."

"Crimea," Englhardt called up, "but we can get back from
Istanbul."

The second man had reappeared on the bridge and for several tense moments they stood there obviously discussing us. I
was beginning to fear that they might send an engineer aboard
to see if they could repair our engine.

"You own that boat?" It was the second man now.

"No, it's owned by a syndicate," I said. "But she's insured."

"Bring her alongside." The man in the dirty tunic called
down to the deck and a moment later a sailor tossed us a line.

"You take care of the rope," I said, hurriedly, in an undertone, "I'll be back in a moment."

I slid down the ladder to the engine room and opened a sea-
cock. They have to take us now, I told myself as I listened to the
water gurgling into the bilge.

Englhardt had fastened the end of the rope to the bow and
they were pulling us over. "Take your time getting up," I whispered when they dropped a rope ladder over the side. "I want her
to fill up before they come and inspect that engine."

He fumbled at the ladder and slowly pulled himself up to
the deck of the tanker. I looped an arm through the ladder, went
forward and unfastened the rope.

"You going to let her go?" The man on the bridge was right over my head.

"Look at her!" I called back. "She's beginning to settle already." I stepped onto the ladder and pushed the *Natasha* off to a watery grave with the wretched thought that I had treated that sturdy little ship very unjustly.

A sailor gave me a hand over the rail. "You are fortunate," he said, grinning at me. "She's going down fast now."

"Yes," I said, "you came along at the right moment." And then, with a tremendous surge of relief, I heard the engine room bell clang and the tanker quiver as she got under way.

We were escorted up to the bridge and discovered that the man in the white tunic was the captain. And less than a minute after we'd met him, Englhardt learned that he was a Christian Democrat, so he told him that he had escaped from a Crimean prison camp and that I was an American and had helped him.

"I wondered why you had opened the sea-cock," he said, turning to me and slowly rubbing his unshaven chin.

I grinned. "I wanted to make sure you'd take us."

"And if I hadn't?" His dark eyes were smiling.

"I'd have had to close the sea-cock and pump her out."

He laughed. "Well, you'll have to do some explaining to the authorities when you land. In the meantime, if you haven't had dinner perhaps you will join me."

"Dinner?" Englhardt rumbled. "We haven't had breakfast yet!"

The *San Giovanni* didn't dock at Istanbul, the captain explained later that evening. Nor was he allowed to discharge passengers there. Which meant, he said, we would have to continue on to Naples, the ship's first port of call. This was all right with me, I assured him, as I was going to Paris. And Englhardt said that since he would have trouble landing without papers anyway, he'd as soon have trouble with the Italians as the Turks—they weren't so close to Russia.

Late the next evening we entered the Bosporus, and as we stood in the bow watching the lights of Istanbul approaching, I asked Englhardt what he planned to do now that freedom was in sight.

"Get some identity papers. And then—" he shrugged "—disappear."

"I think you're wise. I certainly wouldn't hang around Europe. They're going to be looking for you."

"And what will you do?"

"Wind up that ill-fated Luxembourg company. And then get back to work."

"Will you have lost money? You know I still have a good share of the platinum money, and I shall repay you—"

"You'd better hang onto it. You're going to need it. Besides, I doubt if Duchamp will have lost more than that hundred thousand you started it with."

And then for a long time we were silent, staring ahead at the free world. My thoughts were full of this vital personality beside me. I didn't wish to lose sight of him, yet I knew that for his safety as well as mine, we would have to separate for the present, that he would have to go underground. He was too easy to recognize and I had the feeling the Reds weren't going to forget what we had just done to them in a hurry.

At length, he said, "What about the girl, Vera? Are you going to see her again?"

"Oh, I'll look her up when I get to Paris," I replied. "Which reminds me. I wonder if they can send a cable from the ship."

"You wish to tell her you are safe?"

"That we're both safe. I promised." I turned my head and stared at him. "You know, Englhardt, sometimes I have a peculiar feeling..."

He waited for me to continue, but I found it very difficult to express myself, to put into words the thought that had struck me when I first saw Vera in Moscow, that perhaps there was something between these two I didn't know about. Perhaps—and it was not impossible, I reminded myself—that even they didn't know existed themselves.

"You were saying—?"

I turned back to the night "I tell you what—before you disappear, let's the three of us get together in Paris and celebrate."

"Yes," he said with considerable feeling. "That is an occasion I have been looking forward to for some time."

By the time we had passed Istanbul it was nearly midnight and I decided to turn in. For the past hour, Englhardt had been very quiet, watching the lights of the passing port, seemingly lost in thought. I wondered if he was beginning to worry about the last and final stage in his escape to freedom. If the Russians made an international incident out of the affair, he had cause to worry. Embezzlement is a crime in most countries. For that matter it wasn't going to help my commercial reputation any if the true facts of our association became known.

But we still had two or three days ahead of us before he had to face the authorities in Naples. And surely, I told myself, by that time we could develop a story that would satisfy them. I said goodnight and he said that he'd be down later.

I went aft to the tiny two-berth cabin the captain had given us, and soon fell asleep. Sometime later I awakened. The light was still on and his bunk was empty. I got up to switch off the light and saw the note on his pillow. It was hurriedly written in pencil.

Don't worry about me. It's a short swim to shore and if I'm not a good sailor I am an excellent swimmer. I have friends in Istanbul who will take care of me. It is better this way. You will land in Italy without my questionable companionship to make them suspicious of you. And I will not be detained while the authorities decide what to do with me. And so goodbye, my friend.

That's all there was. No hope that we would meet again, nor any clue as to where I could get in touch with him. And characteristically, not a word of thanks. I was reminded of his greeting that first night in Crimea. *I knew you would come but I couldn't stop you.* To Nicholas Englhardt friendship was not a measurable substance to be periodically balanced with a polite phrase.

With the note crumpled in my hand I went out to the stern and gazed back at the loom of the lights of Istanbul. I felt very alone and very depressed. I was sure I would never see him again.

Three days later I landed in Naples without any trouble. The captain had said that in view of Englhardt's disappearance it would be better not to say anything about our escape from Russia. He explained that he would arrange matters with his owners. He was loath to accept it, but I insisted he take five hundred dollars for our passage.

I caught a plane to Paris and immediately went to my apartment. There was no word from Englhardt, not a note telling me that he was safe in Istanbul and I began to worry whether he had made it to the shore that night. Or had he been sucked in by the propellor when he'd jumped over the side?

With mounting anxiety I picked up the telephone and dialed Vera's mother. Mrs. Maudet answered and I explained who I was. Vera, she said, was not there.

"When will she be in?"

"She won't. She left last night for South America."

"South America! Why—I mean—what for?" I stuttered, icy fingers playing with my heart.

"She's going to live there. But don't ask me where. She didn't know herself."

"I don't understand—"

"Nor I." Her voice was petulant. "This giant Russian arrived yesterday morning—I guess they had known each other before—and she said she was going to marry him. I must admit he seemed very nice, but I do think the least she might have done was—"

Softly, I replaced the receiver.

THE END